**"There's more to life than prestige, I guess. . . ."**

Angela raised one slim contoured eyebrow. The man was an enigma. Quitting Smith, Keyes and Lovall with an invitation to return? Her curiosity was aroused. Surely appearing in night court with indigents and helpless old women could not be his main focus.

"I'll do what I can to keep that poor lady from being turned out into the street!"

Rob tossed his shabby briefcase onto the chrome-based, glass-topped table, pushing a futuristic statuette out of the center. Angela grabbed it as it was about to topple.

He winced as she rescued the artwork just before it crashed into the glass. "Sorry. I'm not usually this clumsy. I've had a lot on my mind tonight."

"Well, it seems to have emptied your head of civilities, Mr. Jordan."

"Rob. Call me Rob. And you're perfectly right. I can't even atone for one *faux pas* without committing another." He looked so sincere sorry that Angela laughed in spite of herself. He was certainly a change from her blasé colleagues at Henshaw, Radison and Grimes. Hm, interesting. . . .

# TENDER ADVERSARY

## Judy Baer

Serenade/Serenata
BOOKS
of the Zondervan Publishing House
Grand Rapids, Michigan

TENDER ADVERSARY
Copyright © 1985 by The Zondervan Corporation
1415 Lake Drive, S.E.
Grand Rapids, Michigan 49506

ISBN 0-310-46772-1

Edited by Anne Severance
Designed by Kim Koning

*Printed in the United States of America*

85  86  87  88  89 / 10  9  8  7  6  5  4  3  2  1

*For my parents,*
*Nels and Hazel Fosen*
*with love—*

## CHAPTER 1

"ALL RISE. COURT IS now in session, the Honorable Judge Reynolds presiding."

*Oh, how I hate night court! Everyone is so . . . so common!*

Angela Malone uttered a bored little sigh as she pulled herself from an uncomfortable perch to a standing position. She hated criminal night court. It was so tedious and, well, *pedestrian*. Counselor Malone was thankful that *her* clients rarely found themselves in the pitiful predicaments that landed people here.

Angela tapped one snakeskin-garbed toe against the battered wooden bench ahead of her, her scarlet lip curling in disdain at the accumulation of grime beneath her feet. It was a rare occurrence to find one of Henshaw, Radison and Grimes's promising young attorneys in criminal court defending a client. Angela still resented being the unfortunate one to draw the job.

She pulled her wool wrap close around her as if to shield herself from the disgusting dregs of humanity that surrounded her, and she idly smoothed the black fox trim on her cape.

*It's a good thing I'm wearing black. None of this filth will show. Oh, for a bath and bed!* She tugged impatiently at the hem of her skirt, adjusted the trim-fitting jacket across her shoulders, and smoothed the front of her white silk blouse. Fingering the soft fur strand that ran the perimeters of her cape, Angela shuffled her expensively clad feet.

She was still pondering the insult she felt at being asked to come here to defend the son of her firm's biggest client on a common shoplifting charge, when Judge Reynolds sailed into the courtroom. His robe billowed behind him, much like an improbable, aeronautically unsound kite. Once the judge was ensconced in his chair, she sat down and shrugged deeply into the seat. Her young client shuffled his feet restlessly, the gritty sound grating on her nerves.

"The first case on the calendar this evening is *The State of Illinois v. Mrs. Hannah Green.* Is the State ready?"

There was a scraping of chairs, as one of the State's Attorneys stood to answer. "The State is ready, Your Honor."

"Is Mrs. Green present in the courtroom?"

Silence lay heavy on the stale air. Then low mutters and restless turnings could be heard as those present glanced about, looking for the missing defendant. Suddenly interested, Angela straightened and turned toward the double doors at the back. It was unwise to be late for court. Most unwise.

"Bailiff, will you check the hallway to see if Mrs. Green is present?" Judge Reynolds's face held a frown and his knuckles whitened around the gavel in his hand.

Just then a bright movement near the back of the courtroom caught Angela's eye. The doors swung open, slapping against the wall with a resounding crack. A man strode into the room, suit coat flapping in the self-made breeze. His tie, loose and cocked at a peculiar and unbusinesslike angle, appeared to have been tied on the run. His sandy-brown hair was tousled, and his amazingly bright blue eyes held a look of deep concern.

"Mrs. Green is my client, and she is present, Your Honor. She is still in the hallway."

*My word, he's handsome! What's a man like that doing in a place like this?* Angela sat up, grinning inwardly at the cliché, now interested in the heretofore despicable surroundings. Unconsciously smoothing a scarlet-tipped nail across her sleek black pageboy, she cocked a coquettish eyebrow toward the tall man striding toward the irate judge.

"Mr. Jordan! Must I remind you that you are late? Do you realize that I could hold you in contempt of court?" Judge Reynolds's voice boomed from the bench.

"I'm very sorry, Your Honor, but my client is not well, and I had some trouble getting her here. I thought she could ride comfortably in my car, but as it turned out the vehicle was too small. I finally hired an ambulance to transport her. . . ." The masculine voice trailed off in apology, but then continued more brightly in an appealing little-boy tone, "But we're here *now*, Your Honor."

Much to Angela's amazement, Judge Reynolds merely shook his head and sighed. "Very well, Mr. Jordan. *Don't* let this happen again. Bring her in, and let's get going. I don't want to be here all night."

Angela shuddered at the thought. The only bright spot in the entire room was the handsome attorney who had just entered, and it was apparent that he was incompetent. *Late for court, indeed!*

With a growing awareness that she was in for a long, tedious evening, Angela focused on the one person in the courtroom who would keep her mind off the grubby indigents and long-haired, leather-jacketed youths surrounding her. Her eyes followed his broad back out the courtroom door. Immediately he returned, bent this time over a wheelchair and a frail figure shrouded in blankets. One hand guided the wheelchair, while the other clutched a well-worn leather briefcase. A thick burgundy law book teetered precariously under one arm.

"Are you Mrs. Hannah Green?"

"I am, Your Honor," a quavery voice replied from the wheelchair. Angela could see wisps of white hair haloing a gnomelike bobbing head.

"You're first on the docket, Mr. Jordan. Consider yourself lucky that I've decided not to hold you in contempt of court. Another mistake like this could be very costly for both you and your client."

"Yes, Your Honor. I'm sorry, Your Honor." Mr. Jordan hurriedly steered his charge behind the counsel table. Angela could see the pleased gleam in his eyes as he bent over the frail figure in the wheelchair. It was quite a coup to get away with only a reprimand from Judge Reynolds. He had been sitting at night court for too many years to allow such breaches without good reason.

"The State has indicated that it is ready to proceed. Mr. Jordan, are you and your client ready?"

Angela watched with interest, curious about what would happen next.

Jordan, busy straightening his tie, stood up to face the Judge. Angela noticed that he patted the frail arm of his client before he spoke.

"Your Honor, on behalf of the defendant, Mrs. Hannah Green, I would like to move for a continuance."

*So he's unprepared as well!* Angela's lip curled slightly. Perhaps all he had going for him was his looks. Her own professionalism would never allow her to come into court under such circumstances!

Judge Reynolds, turning to the State's Attorney, queried, "Does the State have any objection?"

Indignation oozed from every pore of the young State's Attorney as he responded. "The State objects on the grounds that Mrs. Green has already delayed a multi-million-dollar office-building construction project by her refusal to obey a duly served notice of eviction, a lawful order of this court!"

"Mr. Jordan, any response?"

"Your Honor, my first contact with my client, Mrs. Green, was at ten o'clock this morning. She was referred to me after she showed her social worker the summons that had been served on her for her appearance here tonight. Although Mrs. Green had, as stated by the State, received a notice of eviction several months ago, she stayed where she was because she did not know what else to do. She has explained to me that she did not move because of her health and the fact that she had nowhere else to go. I do feel, however, that I have found legal justification for her present refusal to be evicted, and that the court should consider reversing its order, which was made at a time when my client was without legal representation." The words flowed smoothly, hinting at real professional savvy.

Angela leaned forward in her seat, electrified by the adroit manner of the man before her. Perhaps there was more to him than first met the eye.

"I need additional time to properly prepare an appropriate motion and supporting legal brief. I do, however, have here with me a photocopy of the case I referred to." With a magician's flair he pulled from his briefcase the stapled copies. Striding to the bench he deposited one copy in the Judge's hands and then turned and gave another to the now rattled-looking State's Attorney.

Duly impressed, Angela began to realize that the handsome attorney was more competent than she had first concluded. He had worked very quickly, under difficult circumstances. *Hannah Green. . . . A construction project. . . .* It all sounded vaguely familiar, but Angela was more curious why the stunning Mr. Jordan was wasting his time and considerable talents on a client who could obviously not afford to pay him.

Judge Reynolds flipped through the photocopied pages while the State fumbled with the transcript. Finally, Judge Reynolds spoke to the State. "Are you aware of this case?

"No, Your Honor." The slump of defeat was evident in the set of his shoulders.

"Based on the probable applicability of this case, the Court will temporarily grant the defendant's motion. Defendant's motion granted." Judge Reynolds's gavel smacked sharply against the desk. "This case will be set on Thursday night of this week at 9:00 P.M. *sharp*," Judge Reynolds shot Mr. Jordan an icy glare, "at which time the defendant and the State shall be prepared to proceed. Next case!" Again the gavel sounded. Angela hurriedly unzipped her portfolio, ready to rise.

Without pause, the court moved on, and Angela heard her case being called.

"*The State of Illinois v. Mr. Kevin Simmons.* Is the State ready to proceed? Is Mr. Kevin Simmons in the courtroom?"

Angela stood and identified herself and her sulky, petulant client, her hand clutching her slim black briefcase.

"Please be seated at the defense counsel table, Ms. Malone, Mr. Simmons."

Angela, leading the way to the front, met Mr. Jordan navigating his client through the swinging doors of the bar. His tie had slipped askew again, and the heavy burgundy law book seemed about to slip out of his grasp. His professional air had vanished and he looked much like a small boy steering a go-cart through a maze. He was so consumed by his progress that he did not see Angela entering the gate. He swung around, clutching his briefcase, and knocked the costly portfolio from her hand.

Legal documents and papers mingled midair and fluttered lazily to the floor. The single latch that had held his briefcase together had come unclasped in the jolt. Angela's open case now dangled from her fingertips, and the tidy, well-organized documents she had compiled blended with his in a heap on the floor.

"Oh, no! How could you?" The words slipped out before Angela could regain her composure.

Apologetic blue eyes met her snapping brown ones.

"I'm sorry, Miss. Apparently I can't walk and drive at the same time!"

He was silenced by an icy stare and dropped to his knees, frantically picking up papers as Judge Reynolds glared at them both in disgust. Shoving papers helter-skelter into her briefcase, Angela made it to the defense table just as the Judge inquired, "Miss Malone, are you ready to proceed?"

"Yes, Your Honor. I'm ready." She shot one final daggered look at the sandy-haired attorney collecting the remaining papers, but he was already smiling sweetly at the elderly lady in the wheelchair before him. Irritation swept through her. Angela seldom went so unnoticed by an attractive man. Shrugging off the affront, she turned to the work at hand.

Her skill held her in good stead as she struggled through Kevin's first appearance. Angela was more rattled by the clumsy encounter with the flaxen-haired man than she cared to admit.

It irked her to be here, defending the fretful, spoiled teenager next to her for shoplifting. The irony was too great. Kevin's father had never once placed blame on the boy for anything his pampered son had done. Until now. But with the boy's latest escapade, a stunt that, embarrassingly, made the morning papers, he had decided that Kevin should be taught to be responsible for his own actions.

"Wealthy Juveniles Caught Shoplifting" the headline had stated. Fortunately, because Kevin was a minor, his name had not been mentioned in the feature article on growing juvenile delinquency in the city. Incensed by the near miss with public humiliation, Milton Simmons had sent him to this court hearing alone, except for Angela, the expensive attorney he had hired.

Milton Simmons was one of Henshaw, Radison and Grimes's biggest and most affluent clients. And in a desperate cry for attention, his son was stealing tennis racquets and balls. The irony was greater still when Angela thought of the double tennis courts and private swimming pool on the Simmons's estate.

The hearing went smoothly, and Angela was relieved to be done. She had gotten Kevin a deferred imposition of sentence. That was as much as she had hoped for. After putting the sullen boy into his father's chauffeured limousine, she walked back into the courthouse to use the telephone. Perhaps her friend Jennifer would be free to drive her home.

"If you're going to call a taxi, don't bother. I can give you a ride."

Angela spun around at the sound of the now-familiar voice. Before her stood the sandy-haired man, tie askew, blue eyes seeming to penetrate her very soul. Suddenly he shot out one long arm.

"Robert Jordan, at your service. Call me Rob. I owe you one for knocking your briefcase onto the floor. I'm really sorry about that."

"Your apologies are accepted, Mr. Jordan. But I prefer to find my own way home, thank you."

"Okay, but we could use the time in the car to sort out our papers."

"*Our* papers? And what is that supposed to mean?"

"Well, they seem to have gotten rather mixed up in

14

the muddle in the courtroom. I have several of your papers, and I know you have a few of mine. I was just going to start separating them. It took quite a while to get Mrs. Green loaded into the ambulance. We can sit here in the corridor and do it. Or you can get home more quickly by sorting them in my car."

Angela weakened. Her apartment was becoming more appealing by the second. Surely it wouldn't hurt to accept a ride. And he seemed harmless enough.

"Oh, I suppose. I am tired. Besides, since you've made a hash of my papers, I'll need to sort through them myself."

"Right! Come on. The car's this way." She followed the broad rolling shoulders through the rear of the courthouse and into the night. Sodium lamps lit the parking lot, bathing the area in an orange glow. Under one light sat a small, battered Volkswagen Beetle with a fender hanging on by sheer will power.

"Here she is! Transportation!" Rob waved at the mangled lump of metal. He bowed and swept open the door to usher her inside.

*And I turned down a ride in the Simmons's limo!* Angela cringed.

Gingerly bending into the interior, Angela was struck with the fragrant smell of earthy, masculine cologne and the tantalizing aroma of popcorn from a half-empty cardboard tub on the floor. Before she was settled, Rob was tugging at the door on the driver's side of the car. With a wrenching of metal, it came open.

"This side sticks a bit. I got sideswiped in college, and it's never been the same." He slid into the driver's seat, filling it with his muscular bulk.

"In college?" Angela mentally tabulated the age of the car and its driver.

"I've had old reliable here since I was eighteen. Now she's ten and I'm twenty-eight. I think I've weathered the years a little better, though. At least I haven't started to rust out!" He turned a sweet, impish grin her way and Angela gave a soft gasp. He had an irrepressible charm that threatened to chip away at her haughty, sophisticated exterior.

The car leapt to life with a shudder and a rumble, and they jerked and lurched out of the parking lot.

"No wonder your client couldn't ride in this thing! If you aren't an invalid when you get in, you will be by the time you get out!" She clung to the dash, her scarlet nails digging in deeply as the car wrenched forward.

"She just has to warm up a bit. Then she runs like a top. Hang on!" Rob pulled into the street, floored the accelerator, and they careened ahead.

Once on the boulevard, the car seemed to settle, and Angela dared speak to its driver once again. "An ambulance is an expensive venture these days. Who do you work for, Rob?"

She saw a flicker of concern pass across his features, but he nodded in agreement and replied vaguely to her question, "I'm self-employed right now. . . ."

With her curiosity piqued, Angela persisted. "And were you employed by a Chicago firm before you set up your own practice?"

Rob squirmed in his seat and muttered, "Smith-Keyes-Lovall."

"What did you say?"

Rob repeated his answer more slowly but with signs of acute embarrassment. "I worked for Smith, Keyes and Lovall."

Angela eyed him thoughtfully. He was being rather humble about having been employed by Chicago's most distinguished and much-touted firm.

"The Smith firm is a very prestigious employer. I'm surprised you left."

"There's more to life than prestige, I guess. They tell me I can come back if I want to, but I doubt that I will. I'm doing what I enjoy right now."

Angela raised one slim, contoured eyebrow in the dark. The man was an enigma. Quitting Smith, Keyes and Lovall with an open-ended invitation to return? A very unlikely situation! Her curiosity was aroused. Appearing with indigents and helpless old women in night court could hardly be his main focus. Before she could ask, he pulled up at the address she had given him.

"Here we are. Did you get the papers sorted?"

"Oh! I completely forgot!" She began to shuffle through the stack in the dark. "I can't see a thing. You'll have to come in, and I'll sort them in the apartment. It will only take a moment."

"Fine. I haven't any other plans. Let me help you out. That door doesn't open from the inside." Rob bolted from the car to the passenger side.

Engaging both hands and one foot to brace himself, he tugged the uncooperative door open, freeing Angela from her metal prison. As she swung her long legs from the car's confines, she noticed with pleasure that Rob was casting an admiring eye from knee to ankle. Her legs were shapely, she knew. At least he had the good sense to notice!

Bestowing a final glare on the persnickety car, she led Rob to the front door of her apartment building. Once off the penthouse elevator, they padded down the heavily carpeted hall. After turning the key in the lock, Angela flung the door open and flipped on the series of lights inside.

They entered the contemporary flat filled with cold, geometric shapes and smooth metals. Pale gray walls and floor enveloped them. Flashes of stark white and midnight black broke the cosmopolitan decor.

"Wow! This is some place!" The stranger seemed as much at home here as he had in the dingy courtroom or the battered car, Angela noted.

"Thank you, Mr. Jordan. Now if you'll lay your papers on the table next to mine, perhaps we can sort them quickly."

"Sure. Anything you say." Rob tossed his shabby briefcase onto the chrome-based, glass-topped table, pushing a futuristic ebony statuette out of the center. Angela grabbed it as it was about to topple.

"I'm sorry! I'm usually not this clumsy! I just have a lot on my mind tonight." He winced as she rescued the artwork just before it crashed into the glass.

"Well, whatever it is, it seems to have emptied your head of civilities, Mr. Jordan!"

"Rob. Call me Rob. And you're perfectly right. I can't even atone for one *faux pas* without committing another!" He looked so sincerely sorry that Angela laughed in spite of herself.

"Come on. Sit down on the couch. I'll scan these papers and get them in order. Would some cappuccino soothe your troubled nerves?"

"Perfect! May I help?"

"No. There are even more breakable things in my kitchen! Besides, it's only big enough for one. These apartments aren't made for cooking." Angela headed for the cubbyhole where she prepared the few meals she ate at home.

"It's a beautiful place, though. Puts mine to shame. But I'm not there enough to notice. I usually don't do anything there but shower and sleep." Rob sank into the white pillowy couch and adjusted several small black throw pillows behind his back.

Angela smiled some moments later as she carried in two cups of steaming cappuccino on a white porcelain tray. Rob had not only made himself comfortable, he had fallen asleep, one sandy forelock over his eye, his head resting against the back of the sofa. Enjoying the view, her eyes followed his finely chiseled profile, rested briefly on the compelling lips, then followed the line of his tie down to a slim, firm waist. His clothes were clean and finely tailored but heavily worn as though he had few changes in his wardrobe.

He had kicked off his shoes. One had pitched

18

sideways, and she could see the well-worn sole in need of mending. She wondered wildly how she had managed to end the evening with this charming, shabbily dressed man sleeping on her couch. His virile masculinity and boyish charm seemed out of place in her stylish, coolly elegant apartment.

"Rob, Rob, wake up!"

"What? Huh? Oh, sorry! Did I fall asleep?" He pulled himself up with a long, leisurely stretch, rubbing his eyes with the heels of his hands. He grinned and yawned like a sleepy tiger. "I've had a hectic few days. Mrs. Green was the icing on the cake. If only she'd called me sooner!"

"I heard you say you'd only met with her this morning."

"At ten o'clock. When she got the eviction notice she didn't know what to do, so she put it in a drawer, hoping it was all a mistake. It wasn't until the summons came that she panicked. She's had no education and no one to look out for her, so I suppose that's understandable. But I had to race to have something ready for tonight. Now I have three days to prepare. That should help."

"I was surprised you found any legal theory to effectively represent her interests on such short notice." Angela commented idly, stirring the dark liquid in the fine porcelain cup before her.

"Frankly, I was too. But as it turns out, I think we have a good argument. I'll do what I can to keep that poor lady from being turned out into the street!" The clear blue eyes turned steely and the soft voice hardened. "I don't see how a developer can tear down hundreds of low-income rental units for an office building and expect those people to find comparable housing elsewhere. At best, it's the destruction of a neighborhood and at worst . . . well . . . never mind. I get all wrought up and you don't want to hear about it." Calm again, he sipped the cappuccino. His eyes twinkled over the brim of the cup.

Angela smiled. She was beginning to enjoy this charming crusader. He was certainly a change from the blasé attorneys she worked with. It was with disappointment that she watched him set down his cup and slip into the discarded shoes.

"Thanks for the coffee and for sorting out the papers. Normally I'm not quite so clumsy." He ran long, sturdy fingers through his hair and ended their trek by massaging the base of his neck. "I'd better get going. I've got lots of research to do."

"Surely, not tonight!"

"Tonight. And every night until Thursday. Mrs. Green is depending on me. 'Bye and thanks. See you in court!" He winked and strode out the door, leaving Angela standing at the threshold watching his receding back. When the outer door swung shut behind him, she turned into the apartment and dejectedly made her way to the sectional.

She could still see the imprint of his body on the white pillows, her only proof that he had been there. He had captured her imagination with his air of sweetness. He was unlike any other man she had ever met; more aggravating, surely, but something else as well—compelling. With thoughts of Rob Jordan flitting in her brain and a smile on her lips, Angela turned out the light and went to bed.

## CHAPTER 2

ANGELA COULD SENSE A nearly palpable tension as she stepped into the offices of Henshaw, Radison and Grimes. Unusual at any time, it was even more uncommon at the sleepy hour of eight A.M. Even the imperturbable receptionist had a wide, excited expression sparkling in her eyes. Miss Martin's salutation hinted at her agitation.

"Welcome to the fireworks, Ms. Malone! Things are really humming here today!"

"Thank you, Lydia. Does this hubbub concern something in which I am involved? Or is everyone simply taking vicarious pleasure in someone else's predicament?" Angela could not keep the sarcasm from her voice. She had always felt that the associates of the firm delighted just a bit too much in the woes of others—especially since the litigation over those woes would pad the firm's bank account.

"All I know is that Milton Simmons called a meeting here and Mr. Henshaw, Mr. Radison, and Mr. Grimes all came for it!"

Angela's eyebrows arched in surprise. The three big

guns did not gather lightly, easily, *or* before 10:00 A.M. unless there was a dire emergency. Squaring her slim shoulders under the simple silk suit, Angela strode purposefully toward her private office.

Whatever the crisis, it could not concern her. Milt Simmons's construction accounts were handled by the senior partners. Her only contact with the family was through Kevin, and she felt freed from responsibility in that area. Her representation of his case in court last night had been flawless.

*A construction company. . . . Hannah Green. . . .* A lone mental note pricked at the strings of her memory. Everything seemed strangely familiar, yet undeniably foreign.

It was not until Pete Wilson sauntered into her office with two cups of steaming coffee and a gossipy smile on his face that the notes fell into place.

"Well, Angela, what do you think of the news? Goliath has been downed by the boy with the slingshot! Or at least the giant is on his knees!"

"Quit talking riddles, Pete. I have work to do. What's going on around here anyway?" Angela tapped the tip of her gold-embossed fountain pen against a crystal ink stand on her desk. Pete was amusing sometimes, but right now his coy manner irritated her greatly.

"So you haven't heard! I thought perhaps you were the one spreading the news, having been there last night!"

"*What* news? What are you talking about?" An ominous tightness was weaving itself about Angela's abdomen. She had a foreboding sense of what was coming.

"About Milton Simmons's construction company and the order to hold up on the new project until some garbage is settled about a homeless little old lady! Simmons evicted her and she didn't go. Now she's got a hotshot lawyer working for her, and the court won't let Simmons's construction crews go ahead until everything is settled. The State couldn't stop him, so now Simmons has pulled us into it. I thought you were there last night when the ruling was made. Every day Simmons delays, it costs him thousands of dollars in interest. And his subcontractors are getting restless. He's livid and biting the tails of everyone in this office. Today was the first time I've ever seen Henshaw *sweat*!"

*Construction. Hannah Green. Of course!* An icy dampness spread across her shoulder blades and down her spine. She could see Hannah Green's blue-veined, gnarled hands and white, bobbing head.

"Angela, are you listening to me? Some unknown attorney with an office address in the crummiest part of Chicago, has put the brakes on a Milton Simmons construction project! His majesty, Mr. Simmons, barrelled into this place in a blue fury and is cheerfully knocking together the heads of the finest legal minds in the state! And you sit there in some kind of a daze! What's wrong with you?"

"What? Oh, yes. Thank you, Pete, for the update." Angela forced herself to move the papers on her desk slowly and methodically to conceal her agitation. "I was there last night, but didn't make the connection with our firm. I didn't realize the project being halted was one of Simmons's. My mind was on my client."

*Kevin.* Another piece in this thorny puzzle was emerging. She had been less than ecstatic when it fell to her to defend Simmons's neglected son who seemed to matter less to his father than a truckload of bricks or an order for concrete beams. The boy's cries for help—vandalism, school absenteeism and finally, shoplifting—had fallen on the indifferent ears of his father.

But Pete persisted in his prattle, unaware of Angela's internal monologue. "So now you know. And this isn't the last of it either, you can be sure."

23

Pete picked up his coffee cup and sauntered toward the door. Before departing, he threw a final comment over his shoulder: "I wouldn't want to be the attorney who's clogged up the works for Simmons. He's going to be steam-rolled into oblivion. Maybe he can be convinced to dump the old dame and we can get on with things." With that Pete left the office, pulling the door shut and leaving a greatly disturbed Angela behind.

Steadying herself, Angela again went through the motions of organizing her already meticulous desk. *Dump the old dame . . . and get on with things.* So that was how Hannah Green was being regarded. Angela could not crush that frail white-haired image in her mind or stifle the rebel thought that Rob should never abandon the poor old lady to the wolves of this firm. Leaving Hannah Green to the legal wiles of Milton Simmons and retinue would be like leading a lamb to the slaughter.

*And Rob! What about Rob?* Angela could only think of him asleep on her couch, vulnerable and unprotected. A sliver of guilt was creeping into Angela's consciousness, for she was beginning to remember why Hannah's name was familiar yet so difficult to place.

Frantically, Angela began to search through the file drawers behind her desk. She flipped through the ivory folders, scanning the headings for what she sought. Simmons. Construction. Evictions. With a sinking sensation, she pulled that last file from the drawer. Opening it to the most recent entry, a name leapt out at her from the list. Hannah Green.

Before her was a notice of eviction that she had drafted for one of the senior partners. Appalled, Angela realized that it was she who had penned the document that had taken Hannah's home from her.

Remembering the day now with vivid clarity, Angela could picture herself thumbing through a vast list of names of those about to receive the notices she was creating. Perhaps that was where Hannah Green's name had come from, sticking itself perversely in her brain, entrenching itself with volumes of other trivia collected by her bright mind.

That draft of an eviction notice had been the last item of business she had put into the Simmons file until her representation of Kevin last evening.

Perplexed and restive, Angela left her desk and entered the corridor that lead to all other parts of the office. From this company artery, she could hear voices drifting from the conference room—some raised in anger, others placating. Inching her way toward the heated sounds, she ashamedly gave in to her curiosity. As she edged nearer the door, she could hear the voice of Milton Simmons railing furiously. From his tone alone, Angela was sure his large-pored, bulbous-nosed face was mottled red in anger.

"Since when does anyone care about these people in those run-down tenements? Some lily-livered, softhearted liberal comes along and tries to save them and what does he get? Nothing, that's what! Helping those people is a waste of time and money. I'd like to know just what that young pup thinks he's doing, coming up against a man like me. I'll ruin him, that's what. That's right. If he doesn't come around to my way of thinking, I'll ruin him!"

The conference door flew open and Angela found herself staring into the popping blue fish eyes of Milton Simmons. His rapid respiration had a raspy sound, as though he were breathing through sandpaper. His protruding stomach met Angela a full second before the rest of his body.

"I want this straightened out immediately! I've got four construction crews sitting on their thumbs while you legal minds hem and haw and say that there's nothing to do but wait. Get rid of this Green woman. Now!"

25

With that, Milton Simmons plowed through the cluster of attorneys who had gathered to witness his tirade. Angela slumped against a nearby wall, drained by the encounter. Rob was up against more than he had bargained for, and she could offer absolutely no assistance.

"Ms. Malone. Come inside, please."

"Yes, Mr. Henshaw. May I help you?" Angela stepped into the confines of the conference room, eyeing the familiar leather chairs that circled a massive oak table. Misters Henshaw, Radison, and Grimes remained seated while the other attorneys filed from the room.

"I'd like to know how your defense of Kevin Simmons is progressing, Ms. Malone."

"Just fine, sir. We worked out a plea agreement with the district attorney to permit Kevin to offer restitution and to perform two weekends of community service." Angela found herself clutching the hem of her jacket with white-knuckled hands. "In exchange, the state accepted a deferred imposition of sentence. Kevin will not have a criminal record if he stays out of trouble for the next six months." Desperately she willed herself not to fidget like a schoolgirl before the principal.

"Keep in mind, Ms. Malone, that *nothing* must go wrong. Milton Simmons is our largest retainer. He has come across some irritants recently that we must resolve for him. Kevin should not be one of them."

"Yes, sir." Angela ground her back molars but managed a stiff smile.

"Good! Just so you understand. We wouldn't want to lose you over a dispute about the Simmons boy, now would we?" Henshaw's smile stopped at his lips. His eyes were cold and calculating. The message was clear. If Simmons lost, so did the firm, and more directly, so did she. Angela departed, her professional demeanor still intact. It was her insides that had begun to revolt. Waves of uneasiness crested and broke within her.

Henshaw's threat was obvious. Milton Simmons had to be appeased on some fronts—especially that of his son. Angela's relief at being far removed from the situation had disappeared. In its place was the fearful feeling of sitting in the eye of a storm, waiting for it to burst upon her again—full force.

*Rob.* They were gearing up to do battle against Rob and the pitiful, homeless Hannah Green. Those two innocents would not even know what hit them. And Angela knew with a deep sadness that she could not help them. Her position at Henshaw, Radison and Grimes was too valuable to be risked. Her tastes were too expensive, her palate, too well trained.

Putting the muscular, sandy-haired man from her mind was not the simple task she had hoped it would be. Each time her eyes left the legal tomes before her to search the sky outside her window she was reminded of his eyes, clear and penetrating as the cloudless expanse before her. With every legal notation penned, she remembered the legal wiles he had displayed to obtain a continuance for Hannah's case. And without reason at all, she would conjure up the image of him asleep on her couch, radiating puppy-dog charm and consummate masculinity.

By day's end, Angela was tired and vaguely depressed. She wearily pulled her leather portfolio from her desk. Working at home seemed the only answer. She coveted the silky softness of her bed and the comforting closeness of the canopy that surrounded it. She would work there, in her haven away from this frenetic office.

Pulling at the documents in her case, she came across a note on yellow legal paper in a firm bold script very unlike her own fine scrawl. Before her was a case-by-case listing of Rob's research—the case notations to be used in Hannah Green's defense.

Suddenly the day brightened. She held in her grasp an excuse to see Rob again. Inexplicably refreshed, Angela began to shove papers into the slim portfolio. She was surprising even herself. Angela was not usually so forward with men. Why should she be? After all, they always sought her out.

Another errant thought came to her mind. Perhaps this was a means whereby she could help to settle her firm's predicament as well. Angela nurtured the secret hope that she could dissuade Rob from pursuing Mrs. Green's case. If she couldn't forestall trouble, it was going to be a nightmare around the office. Milton Simmons would see to that.

Simmons was spoiled, petulant, and cruel when crossed. Rob's muddled sweetness was no match for that. Tangling with Simmons was like crossing a tightrope without a net. There were no second chances. Simmons could ruin him—or her entire firm.

Eager to be on her way to Rob, Angela slipped into the hallway hoping to travel unseen to her low-slung black sports car in the parking lot.

She cursed softly under her breath as she heard Pete's cheerful salutation behind her. "Hey! Angie! Where are you hurrying off to? Want to go have a drink with me?"

"You know better than that, Pete. It clouds the mind and squanders my precious calories. Anyway, I have other errands to run." Angela's straight nose wrinkled in distaste at Pete's suggestion.

"I know, I know. You always say that. See you tomorrow!"

Her eyes followed Pete's suit-clad form down the hall and came to rest on the farthest door. The words *Word Processing* were emblazoned on the clouded glass.

Tightening her grip on the slim portfolio, Angela followed the lead her legs were taking until she stood in front of the very door to which her eyes were riveted. An idea, though not quite ethical or fully formed, was beginning to bloom in her fertile brain.

Suddenly, Angela slipped stealthily through the door and made her way to the photocopy machine purring in the corner. With one swift motion, she pulled Rob's case list from her briefcase and threw it onto the glass table of the copier. With the punching of a button and a flash of light, the page was duplicated.

*I'll keep this . . . just in case. I won't even study it. Not now. Maybe that won't be necessary.* Fingers of guilt prodded at her conscience, but now she was assured knowledge of Rob's position of attack on the Simmons and Green case. It might be useful if Henshaw's threats came to fruition.

Hurriedly shoving the paper from sight, Angela smoothed her dark pageboy and strode from the room, her posture daring anyone to question her purpose for being there.

As she distanced herself from the office in her Mercedes, her guilt at copying Rob's work diminished and her enthusiasm at seeing him grew again. She smiled to herself in the rear-view mirror and was surprised at the lively eyes that glowed back at her. Angela had nearly forgotten the excitement of teenage infatuation. Tickles of excitement fluttered inside, like butterfly wings, and she gaily hugged her elbows to her ribs as she drove in a vain effort to quell the anticipation she was experiencing. Rob Jordan had mined a facet of her character long buried.

She relished the wind whipping through her inky black hair as she sought the address of one Robert Jordan, Attorney at Law. Soon, however, the delight turned to alarm, as the freeways turned into streets, and the streets into alleyways and the alleyways into ominous tenements with dejected looking residents on stoops and small groups of youths breakdancing on the corners.

Pulling up in front of Rob's office, Angela gave a shudder of dismay. Peeling paint and broken windows marred the front of a once gracious building, and a large dead rat lay stiffly on the bottom step.

"Hey, lady! You lookin' for me?"

Angela's eyes darted in fright to the unlocked passenger door of her car and fell on a strong hand reaching to grip the handle. She smothered the gasp of fear rising in her throat just as an attractive face with sandy hair and blue eyes followed that hand into her line of vision.

"Rob! You scared me half to death!"

"I should have. What are you doing in a neighborhood like this, Miss Malone? It's not very wise to be down here alone—especially with your car doors unlocked."

"I was looking for you. We didn't do a very thorough job of sorting our papers, after all. I found another sheet of yours in my portfolio this morning."

"Whew! It's my case listing, isn't it?" Rob's features radiated relief. "I was afraid that I would have to do that work all over again. Thanks for bringing it over! Do you have time to come into my office? I'd like to show you around." Then he hastened to add, "It's not as classy as your firm, but it's the best in this neighborhood."

"I'd love to. I don't believe I've ever been in this part of Chicago before." Angela slipped a smoky-stockinged leg out of the sleek car and gingerly set a leather pump on the littered pavement.

"No one ever comes to this part of the city to visit. It's a good place for leaving, not coming to." Rob strode around to the driver's side and ushered Angela out onto the street and toward the soot-encrusted, ill-kept building.

He kept up a running patter as he herded her through the clutter to his office.

"Don't step on the pets," he quipped as they

skirted the offending corpse of the rat, "and watch for falling glass."

Angela's slim body started as a free-flying baseball shattered a window above her. Rob threw a protective arm over her head and shoulder and pushed her through the door into a gloomy foyer.

"How can you stand it here?" Angela gasped. "It's simply dreadful! How could you leave Smith, Keyes and Lovall for *this*?"

An equable grin met her distraught gaze. "Actually, for me it was more of a question of how I could *stay* with them as long as I did."

Stunned to silence by his vague, enigmatic answer, Angela followed Rob's broad back up the dimly lit stairs to his office.

"Well, here it is! Come on inside!" He threw open the door and Angela had to suppress a gasp of amazement at the contrast that confronted her.

Inside was a highly scrubbed office, painted in peaceful shades of green. Sunshine yellow cabinets and bright bold poster art splattered color about the muted room. A dark-haired, olive-skinned girl sat behind the receptionist's desk, tapping diligently at a small word processor.

"Do you like it?" Rob's voice was only inches from her ear.

She turned to face him, tilting her head toward his, her inky hair flowing from her visage in a charcoal wave. "It's like an island in the storm! How . . . why . . . ?"

"I think my clients deserve it. They don't have many places to come and feel special, Angela. So I've made this one. It's mostly a matter of keeping things clean." Rob wandered around the room running a finger over the spotless files and sills. "If a person's self-respect is left intact they will try the best they can with what they have. I have three of the most diligent cleaning ladies in the city—all working two shifts a week to clean my office in payment for services rendered. They'd wash my clothes and give me a bath if I'd let them. It's a first for any of them to know they have access to legal service and a method of paying the bills.''

"Why?"

"Why what?" Rob spun to face her, a quizzical expression on his features.

"Why? If you can manage this . . . oasis . . . in the middle of a ghetto and make it work, why didn't you stay with the big firms and pull in the money that goes with the territory?'' She stood with hands splayed, puzzling out an answer.

"They don't need me there, Angela. What kind of a service do I perform for diamond-draped matrons wanting to sue their caterers for substituting black lumpfish roe for prestige caviar? Those people don't need my help. But the ones here do.''

Angela's dark eyes widened at the passion in Rob's voice, and through her brain marched a series of her own clients in their Dior suits and Gucci accessories.

Before she could speak, the outer door opened, and a small woman, stooped beyond her years, entered. A large-eyed child clung to her skirt.

"Mr. Jordan?"

"Hello, Estine, did you get another letter from the welfare office?" Rob left Angela's side to greet the woman, taking her dirt roughened hand in his own.

"They scare me, Mr. Jordan. I can't understand all the words, but they scare me. Does this mean I can't get help for my little Amanda?" She clutched the letter in her fist, crinkling the missive in her alarm.

"You'd better let me read it and decide." Rob glanced over the crumpled page. "This is just a form letter, Estine. It's simply telling you that there will be a hearing next week. It gives the welfare office the opportunity to voice any objections it might have. But I doubt there will be any. Would you like me to be there—just in case?''

"Oh! Could you?"

"I think so. Here, let me write it in my appointment book so I don't forget." Undaunted by the unavailability of a secretary, Rob slid into the vacant chair and added Estine's hearing to the list of appointments and obligations.

Angela sat back in a lemon-yellow plastic chair and watched Rob function. It was more than law in which he dealt. Patience and gentleness simply radiated from him.

But her puzzlement grew. Though she was beginning to see some minute intangible rewards in this mission-type legal work of his, she could not begin to imagine how Rob was financing his situation. That hit Angela full force when her dark eyes caught him in the act of slipping the pitiful Estine a twenty-dollar bill from his own wallet.

A weight of obligation began to fall upon her. She had to convince Rob that this was foolishness! He could be as generous as he wanted with these nondescript, unimportant people as long as he abandoned Hannah Green. If he didn't do that, Milton Simmons would put a stop to this sunshiny office and the charity that Rob seemed so bent on doling out!

"Rob. I need to talk to you."

"Okay. I'm sorry. I didn't mean to get so involved. Most people who come here aren't accustomed to making appointments, so I have just fallen into the habit of working with them as they arrive. I normally don't have a beautiful woman waiting in the wings." He flashed a wide, toothy grin chock full of charm and nearly dashed her resolve to scold him.

"I've been worrying about something all day, Rob, and now we've got to talk."

33

"So talk away." He sprawled into the chair facing hers, his long legs stretched before him. He loosened his tie and let it rest askew under one ear and folded his long, well-shaped hands across a trim torso.

"Rob, give up Hannah Green as a client."

The only outward response Angela could detect was a tightening of his folded hands. His voice was as pleasant and easy as before.

"No. I can't do that."

"Rob! Milton Simmons is a brute! He'll make sure you're done for in this town if you go up against him over this eviction notice!"

"I won't lose any of the clients I have now."

"Nonpaying clients, you mean!"

"Well, true; a good share of my clients are nonpaying."

"You're crazy, Rob! Why tackle Simmons over one little old lady?" Angela was fighting to keep the anger from her voice, but he seemed oblivious to her arguments.

"Why shouldn't she count as much as Milt Simmons or you or I? What makes her less special, Angela?"

"She's not less special, really, she's just . . ."

"Poor?"

"That's not fair, Rob!" Angela protested.

"Exactly what I'm saying. It's not fair that she not have adequate representation just because she's poor. And I'll provide it for her—whatever the cost to myself."

Angela threw up her hands in frustration. There was something about this man that she simply couldn't understand. Characteristically curious, she became determined to find out what is was. Whatever motivated Robert Jordan was more powerful than anything she had ever experienced, more powerful even than the lure of wealth.

But was there anything more powerful than that?

34

# CHAPTER 3

"DINNER?"

"What?" Angela started and her dark eyes flew to
Rob's amused blue gaze.

"Dinner. With me. Will you have dinner with me?"
He was uncoiling his muscles in a leisurely catlike
stretch and grinning as he watched her, waiting for an
answer. His biceps flexed as he bent his arms double
over his head and then stretched them ceilingward,
yawning widely. His trim torso appeared sleek and
sinewy beneath his thin cotton shirt. Angela's eyes
swept from the firm expanse of his chest to the
elongated profile of his legs as he completed his
exercise. As her eyes finally ended their trek at his
lips, he spoke.

"All this legal quibbling makes me tired, Angela.
Let's go have dinner. I don't think I remembered to
eat today. I could use a meal."

Coyly Angela acquiesced, but she caught the
triumphant gleam of her own eye in the mirror over
the secretary's desk. A dinner invitation was exactly
what she'd hoped for. Rob was so reserved and

gentlemanly that she'd begun to wonder if he saw something wrong in her. Other men she had known made advances far more quickly than he.

"All right, though I can't imagine why I'm agreeing—we haven't concurred on anything else today. I do have to go back to my office, however. I left a file on my desk that I need for tonight. I planned to finish some work at home and I've just remembered it. I'll meet you at the restaurant. Name a place."

A hint of concern flickered in Rob's eyes, but the moment was so fleeting, Angela at once thought she had imagined the troubled look.

"Is Rimaldi's okay with you? The food's good even if the atmosphere isn't much." His tone was faintly apologetic as he suggested a moderately priced street-side café.

Used to more lavish cuisine and a richer ambience, Angela struggled to keep a placid expression in place. "Rimaldi's is just fine. I'll meet you there in half an hour."

"Okay, lady lawyer. See you then."

Angela watched Rob in her rear-view mirror as she pulled away from the dingy building that housed his office. As the sleek black Mercedes departed, a grubby, barefooted child raced up to Rob, hands stretched upward, begging to be lifted into his arms. Angela could see him comply as she turned the corner to make her way out of the perverse maze that led to this pitiful place.

Back at her office, Angela raced past the security guard into her own sanctuary. Lifting the file from her desk, she paused before leaving, allowing her eyes to drift around the room in which she had spent such an important portion of her life.

Her gaze rested on a teak curio cabinet full of delicately carved figurines of ivory and wood—one-of-a-kind creations she had collected from her own extensive travels and from the rare client who thought to show appreciation for her work in a more intimate and tangible way. Following the line of the cabinet to its base, she detachedly observed the hand-tied Oriental rug on which it rested. On more than one long, weary night, she had kicked off her impractical and uncomfortable shoes to curl them in the decadently satiny cushion.

Silk-screened prints, original oils, and numbered lithographs littered the walls of her office. Imposing antique bookcases held several gold-embossed antique books from her own personal library as well as the scores of legal volumes her profession required.

With all the obvious luxury, something was missing. Her leather wing-backed chairs seemed no more appropriate than those of yellow molded plastic in Rob's sparse office. Her carefully crafted, exquisitely chosen artwork gave her office no more soul than the bright and splashy dime-store posters hanging from Rob's painted walls. A realization came to her like the proverbial lightning bolt. Her office was all show, while Rob's was full of heart.

Rattled by the philosophical turn her mind had taken, Angela searched for a distraction. Spying the door of her closet ajar, she strode toward it hurriedly, glad for a new purpose. Whipping through the extra items of clothing she stored there for just such circumstances, she pulled a deep blue-green camisole from its hanger and a new pair of hose from an adjoining shelf.

Sliding out of her dusky nylons, she slipped her toes into the sheer silk hose she had been saving for a festive occasion. Admiring the long length of her shapely calves in the mirror, she straightened the seamed hose into parallel lines, adjusting the tiny silk bows woven into the fabric at the heel. Tossing her jacket across the back of a winged chair, she slipped out of her now wilted blouse. After tugging the teal camisole over her head and tossing her hair until it glinted into place like a black wave, she viewed herself critically in the mirror.

Rob would like what he saw. He *had* to. She was a composite creation of the finest and most expensive designers, hairdressers, and make-up artists in the city. Though pleased with the dark-haired reflection, Angela could not shake the feeling that Rob was looking for something more—maybe something within her. What, she was not sure. Something she could not provide. Not yet, anyway.

Locking a glistening row of pink-hued pearls around her neck, Angela hurried from her office. She was late. Rob would be wondering what had happened to her.


The tiny sidewalk café was teeming with patrons, most of whom were college students, when Angela raced to the gaily canopied entrance.

"Excuse me, I'm supposed to meet someone . . ."

"Ms. Malone? Mr. Jordan's on the first terrace, near the back." The host was courteously pointing the way as Angela realized how at home Rob must be in this quaint little place.

He was deeply engrossed in the menu as Angela approached, oblivious to the music and noise surrounding him. A worried frown furrowed his brow, and for the first time since they had met, he looked older than his years.

It dawned on her then, that perhaps dinner even here was a financial burden on Rob's already strained pocketbook. His eyes were following the price-list down the right hand column of the page rather than the food selections on the left. Sensing her presence, the frown eased and he looked up.

"Angela! Hi! I was beginning to think we'd gotten our signals crossed. . . . Boy! Do you look nice!" Rob stood, the filigreed iron chair scraping backward as his legs made contact with its base.

"Thank you. I decided to freshen up a bit. I'm sorry I'm late."

"No problem. I memorized the menu while I was waiting. What would you like?"

"Rob, . . . maybe you'd rather not . . . eat out tonight." She remembered the twenty-dollar bill he had furtively passed to his client.

"Well, it's this or starve. I haven't been grocery shopping in a week. Aren't you hungry?"

"A little. What do you recommend?" If he was determined to eat, she wouldn't stop him.

"The lasagna is good. So is the fettucini al fredo. The ravioli is passable and the clam sauce terrible."

"Sounds like you frequent this place."

"Faithfully. It's only a short walk from my apartment and just as cheap, uh, easy, as cooking at home."

Catching his slip of the tongue, Angela resolved herself to a new experience. It had been a long time since she had been in the company of a man with the finances of a college student. She had sworn off them long ago, as soon as she discovered that they were ineffectual stepping stones to her success. Older, richer men were more her style. Still, she found herself comfortable in Rob's amiable, poverty-stricken company.

It was not until a waiter in a red-and-white checked apron set before them two steaming bowls of minestrone, that Angela realized just how out-of-tune she and her companion really were. As the spicy smells wafted into her nostrils, Angela closed her eyes, savoring the heady, hearty flavors. When she opened them, they fell on Rob, his head bowed in prayer over the thick pottery bowls and baskets of crusty bread.

Unnerved, Angela self-consciously picked up a spoon and dropped it again, uncharacteristically unsure of her next move. Shortly Rob's eyes opened and he grinned in awareness of her discomfiture.

"You don't have to wait for me, Angela. The soup's getting cold."

"Yes, well, I thought . . . never mind." She attacked the steaming broth with an intensity born of acute self-consciousness. Rob Jordan had a way of putting her off balance with everything he did. *Praying in public! How humiliating!*

Racking her brain for a suitable topic of conversation, Angela grasped the first available straw.

"Did you say that you lived near here?"

"Yup. Only two blocks away. It's a college neighborhood, full of loud music and all night parties, but I like it. It's a nice change from the section of town my office is in. All I hear over there are police sirens and gang fights."

"How can you stand it, Rob? It's so *depressing!*"

"That's where my clients are, Angela."

"Your clients! Really, Rob! Be sensible! Clients are people who *pay* you for services rendered. Those people belong at Legal Aid Services. What you have going is *charity work!*" Angela's lip curled in derision.

"Is that so bad?" Rob put both forearms on the tablecloth before him and studied her closely, his head cocked appealingly to one side.

"So bad? It's awful, Rob! What kind of people come through your office? Welfare cases, juvenile delinquents, old women who don't have enough sense to know what an eviction notice means! You can't earn a living that way. There are government services for that type of person. Let them use welfare and Legal Aid. You're bright, well-educated, promising. Why waste it in some slum when you could have wealth, power, whatever you wanted?" Angela's tirade ground to a halt as she realized what a harridan she must seem.

Rob's expression had changed little. It was apparent that he had heard all this before.

Quietly he began to speak, quoting phrases foreign

to Angela's ears. "Consider your call, brethren; not many of you were wise according to worldly standards, not many were powerful, not many were of noble birth; but God chose what is foolish in the world to shame the wise, God chose what is weak in the world to shame the strong, God chose what is low and despised in the world, even things that are not, to bring to nothing things that are, so that no human being might boast in the presence of God. . . . Let him who boasts, boast of the Lord."

Stunned, Angela simply stared at the man across from her. He gazed back through peaceful blue eyes, smiling slightly, unoffended by her tirade.

Suddenly, Angela felt as if she were treading on treacherous, forbidden ground. She did not understand this side of Rob Jordan. She felt as lost as if she had come into court unprepared. Her heartbeat quickened and she felt a surge of racing adrenaline, but she could not find a response for his amazing quotation.

She stared at him blankly, a sneer pulling at the corner of one lip, her quick mind cataloging history's philosophers for a familiar niche in which to house the quotation. *Is he spouting Plato, Aristotle, or Shakespeare—or trying to enroll me in some funky philosophy class?* Suspiciously, she blinked. *Now she remembered. She had heard this type of stuff from people handing out tracts.*

"First Corinthians One, verses twenty-six through thirty-one," he added.

"What did you say?" she queried, still off guard.

"The Scripture reference for those verses. It's in Corinthians. Apropos, don't you think?"

Speechless, Angela laid down the soup spoon she had been clutching and shook her head from side to side. Covertly, she realized that she was glancing to the right and then the left, hoping that no one she knew had heard that little spiel of Rob's. This

Christianity of his was embarrassing as well as confusing!

"I'm a Christian attorney, Angela, no matter how many people think that might be a contradiction in terms. And it's my business to help people—no matter who they are or what their status." And as quickly as the sermonette had begun, it ended. "Enough of that for now, don't you think?" Rob was grinning again, that blatantly sensual grin that made her heart lurch in her chest.

Forgiving him instantaneously for whatever imagined embarrassment he could potentially have caused her, she plunged her spoon back into the cooling soup. Even such strange topics of conversation could not totally mar the delight in being with this charming, unpretentious man.

Much to her surprise, Angela found herself enjoying the simple meal. Though accustomed to more lavish fare, she did not miss her normal crab salad garnished with golden caviar or tiny potful of rich lobster bisque.

"Are you ready for dessert?"

"You must be kidding! I'm so full of pasta I can hardly move!" Angela patted the waistband of her skirt in mock horror.

"Then come over to my place. The one thing I do have in my refrigerator is spumone. I'm an addict. You can't end an Italian dinner without a dish of spumone!" Rob stood and extended a hand, which Angela willingly grasped.

It was just too tempting. As much as her logic warned her against it, she wanted to visit Rob's apartment and to see where he lived. Rob Jordan could do nothing to further her career. He might even be the very man to jeopardize it, but she could not seem to stay away.

"Perhaps you should drive over. I wouldn't want you walking back for your car late at night. Even this neighborhood has its problems."

"Am I planning to stay late into the night?" Angela asked with a playful coyness she had not felt since her teens.

"You never know." The deep, brooding expression in his eyes made tingles of excitement play along Angela's spine. Feeling very much like a girl on her first date, she nestled her hand into his larger one and let him lead her docilely to the car. Inwardly she smiled. This was more what she had expected of the evening!

Another surprise lay in store for her at Rob's apartment. Though the rooms were faintly shabby, what little furniture he owned was richly elegant and bespoke quiet good taste. Two Frank Lloyd Wright chairs flanked a sleek Parsons table, and three contemporary chairs padded with oriental futons lined one wall. The thin, bendable mattresses took the place of a davenport. Through the bedroom door, Angela could see a king-sized water-bed filled with downy comforters and fluffy pillows. On the blank white walls, Rob had painted geometric designs. A bold rust and navy arrow circled around the room's circumference, from wall-to-ceiling to wall-to-floor, meeting itself as both ends of the arrow ended in a large rust vase filled with dried plants.

"Rob! What a wonderful place! This furniture is incredible!"

"All I can take credit for is the bed and the paint on the walls. That's what I was living with until my mother came to visit. Next thing I knew she had sent me a truckload of her 'least promising' items to 'camp out' with."

"These are her 'least promising' pieces?" Angela commented dryly. "She must have quite a house!" Angela's practiced eye could spot quality. And Rob's apartment fairly radiated with it.

"My mother is an interior decorator. Furniture

43

moves faster through our home than through a retail outlet. If she remembers one of these pieces when she's doing another house, it will be gone—just like that. I've never been one to become attached to 'things.' They can always be replaced."

Sticking his head into the freezer portion of the refrigerator for a moment, Rob suddenly popped out, frosty steam circling his head like a halo.

"Here it is—spumone ice cream. Three scoops or four?"

"Hold it! I just want a taste. I'd rather just sit here and enjoy the furniture. It's gorgeous!"

"You can't eat furniture. If you'll excuse me, I'll entertain myself with something more tasty."

Soon Rob joined her on the futons-cum-couch where she had curled into a ball, resting her head against the creamy cushion. She eyed him from her cozy vantage point, mentally willing him to her side of the couch. She could sense his reservation and it worried her. Perhaps all he needed was a little encouragement. He smiled as she edged toward him on the rickety settee, and when she theatrically licked her lower lip and eyed the bowl in his hand, he held a spoonful of the ice cream to her lips, lightly touching the icy, sugary sweetness to them. Angela opened her eyes, grinned slightly and licked the tip of the spoon.

Rob watched her, relishing the dainty feline movements, reminded of a haughty kitten willing to pounce or purr on a moment's notice. His eyes followed the gentle relief of her features, caressing each lovely shadowed recess of the classic face, admiring the gentle turn of her ivory cheek and the dusky outline of her dark eyes.

Her eyes. He could catch a glimpse of some haunting inner fire in their depths. They were eyes like none other—wise, knowing, and strangely innocent, showing a beguiling purity of spirit that belied the sophisticated armor she wore so well.

So defensive, yet defenseless. With her nearness, Rob felt the urge to surround her, shelter her, separate her from whatever demons drove her to achieve.

His breath sharpened as he fought the overwhelming need to claim her as his own. As she snuggled nearer, his mind raced with a question he had seldom considered, seldom asked. "Is she the one, Lord? Is this the woman You meant for me?"

As Rob sought a will beyond his own, Angela nestled closer and the ice cream was forgotten. She found herself wrapped in his strong arms, her head resting against his shoulder. Placing his chin atop her sleek hair Rob shattered his own introspection.

"You know, this is better than the spumone!"

Laughing, Angela sat up slightly, turning toward him to counter the teasing, when she found herself only millimeters from his face. Slowly, time suspended, their profiles met. His lips captured hers in a leisurely, intoxicating kiss.

Before she had time to recover, however, she found herself being dumped unceremoniously onto the highly polished hardwood floor. Rob came sliding after her as the cushions of the makeshift couch avalanched over the couple, entangling them in a mound of soft mattresses.

Angela could hear a soft, disgusted mutter near her ear. "Fooey. I knew I should have fixed the leg on that end chair!" After some rodentlike scrambling on the distant side of the cushion, it folded down to reveal a tousled head and bright blue eyes. An even, amused grin soon followed.

"Broken leg. I told you these were my mother's less promising pieces."

The two bodies began to quiver, nearly imperceptibly at first, rising to a hilarious crescendo as the two imprisoned in the tangled clutter of mattresses began to laugh. Angela could feel the warm bursts of Rob's breath against her cheek as the ludicrousness of the situation hit him. She joined him, the peals of laughter finally rocking their bodies until both lay back, holding aching ribs against the onslaught.

"Rob, help me out of here!" Angela kicked ineffectually at the bendable cushions cascading around her and wiped the tears of laughter from her dark lashes.

"That implies I can untangle myself first! My trousers seem to be caught on the broken leg of this chair. . . ." The rending of fabric pierced the air and the two convulsed in laughter again as Rob finally stood displaying a jagged trouser leg.

He reached forward and offered Angela both hands, pulling her upright from the wreckage.

"Don't go telling anyone else how romantic I am. I don't want women beating down my door for an experience like this one." His wry voice came to her as he bent over to examine the damage to his pants and the wooden frame that had held the futon.

"Never. I want this to be a once-in-a-lifetime experience." Angela gasped, tears of laughter blinding her.

"Me too. Not only did my chair break, my trousers rip and the ice cream land on the middle of one of these dumb cushions, I have achieved a record for *faux pas* in a three-minute period!"

Startled by the physical impact he was able to have on her, she fluttered away from the offending couch, marking time until her composure returned. Reminding herself for the hundredth time that Rob Jordan could be her enemy if he persisted in defending Hannah Green, Angela mentally doused ice water on her smouldering emotions.

Struggling to keep her tone light, she edged toward the door as she spoke. "Now that we've had all this fun, I think I'd better be running along. It's been . . . uh, an experience."

"Leaving so soon? What if I had a finale planned?

You know, something like a wall caving in or the ceiling dropping on our heads? Are you sure you have to leave . . ." his finger stroked the soft curve of her cheek, " . . . and miss all the excitement?" Angela read the tender message in his eyes. Rob was as attracted to her as she was to him. Danger signals flashed in her brain. Until the Simmons and Hannah Green case was behind them, Rob Jordan should be off limits. Mr. Henshaw's warning words marched through her mind.

*"Keep in mind, Ms. Malone, that nothing must go wrong." Nothing must go wrong . . . with her defense of Kevin or with the firm's handling of Milt Simmons's affairs.* Rob had placed himself in the middle of it all by defending Hannah Green. Her legal conscience was doing war with her emotions. She wanted to stay, she needed to go. Nothing must go wrong. . . .

"Rob, can I stay a moment? I think we should talk."

"About what, Angela? You can talk to me about anything—except Simmons and Hannah Green—and I have a feeling that's what's on your mind."

"Please, Rob. Just stay out of this thing with Simmons. He's a man-eater."

"And I presume he downs an occasional woman, too?" Rob's pointed question struck to the heart of the matter. Angela hung her head. "What effect does this have on you? If I win this thing for Hannah Green, what does it do to you?"

"I don't really know at this point, Rob." Angela's voice was soft, unsure. "I've been warned by Mr. Henshaw that nothing is to go wrong in the defense of Kevin Simmons, Milton's son."

"Is that the boy you had in night-court? The miserable-looking kid?"

"Yes. He's been neglected and pushed aside for so long, I doubt he can be straightened out now."

"There's always hope, Angela, but let's get back to you. Is the firm looking for a scapegoat in case this whole mess blows up in its face?" Rob's finely chiseled features creased in genuine concern. The caring look struck the telling blow to Angela's weakening armor. He had put into words the very fear she had been harboring ever since her brief meeting with Mr. Henshaw.

"I'm afraid of it, Rob. Terribly afraid. I've distanced myself from Milton Simmons for some time now, and just when I want to be far away from any of his dealings, Henshaw reels me back through this appearance with Kevin. I'm the newest and youngest associate—and the most dispensable. If heads must roll, I think mine will be first." Tears sprang to Angela's eyes. Expressing the burden she had been carrying was not easy. She'd kept no counsel but her own—until now. And for reasons she could not define, she was pouring out her soul to the very man who might cause her heartache.

"I'm sorry, Angela. I really am." Rob appeared to be genuinely apologetic. Perhaps there was hope, after all.

"Then drop this thing with Hannah Green! Let Simmons build his building! I'll help you find a place for Hannah. Please?"

"I can't. You know that. And it's not just Hannah. There are lots of people who are homeless because of this project. Something needs to be worked out. Just stay clear of the Simmons affair."

"And *I* can't do that! I'm the only thing between Kevin Simmons and reform school. If I fail, Milt Simmons will have me out on my ear. I'm a whole lot less valuable to Mr. Henshaw than the Simmons account!"

"Would you let me help?"

"What do you think I've been asking of you Rob? Of course you can help—drop the suit!"

"Not that. But I could help with Kevin. Maybe we could get him into counseling and a work program of some sort. Just to keep him off the streets and out of jail. If he pulls another stunt like stealing or vandalism, he'll be behind bars. If we can keep him clean, Henshaw can't put the finger on you."

Angela's eyes brightened behind the threatening tears. The suggestion made sense. Kevin was her only connection to the Simmons case. Even if Rob did win his suit, as long as she helped his son, Milton Simmons would want her in the firm. An ironic smile touched her lips. The only way to save her own neck was to help someone else save his. It would be a new experience, trying to salvage a young boy's tumultuous life. But Rob seemed confident that it could be done.

The specter of the dead rat and broken glass materialized in her brain. Rob should know what could be done in impossible situations.

"Angela! You forgot this."

Turning sharply, wondering what she had left behind, she came full face with Rob who bent over her, kissing her with a gentle force that left her reeling. An idle thought drifted through her mind as she lost herself in the moment. Here was one part of Rob's life in which nothing was shabby, nothing was wanting. He had the ability to erase her mind, making a clean slate, empty of any thoughts but those he cared to write on it.

Still savoring the sweet and salty taste of his lips on hers, Angela groped her way to the door.

"G'night, Angie."

Unable to correct even the irritating abbreviation of her given name, Angela waved a limp hand and escaped into the hallway, still astounded by her attraction to this enigma of a man.

## CHAPTER 4

"I WONDER WHAT THAT FOOL is up to now?"

"It sounds as if he's about to dig himself into a hole he won't get out of!"

"Do you think he's crazy enough to pursue this?"

"Nah. I think he just wants to give Simmons a scare before he drops it."

"Well I think he's just too dumb to know better. Have you ever seen the section of town his office is in? What good can come out of there?"

Angela slipped quietly into the ladies' room, anxious not to be caught eavesdropping on the two attorneys strolling down the hall in front of her. She normally had no interest in the scuttlebutt around the firm, but ever since Rob Jordan's name had begun cropping up she found herself poised with ears alert for any mention of his name.

The consensus was that Robert Jordan was an idiot to take on Milton Simmons and the firm of Radison, Henshaw and Grimes. But he *had* managed to obtain a temporary restraining order at his Thursday-night hearing, grinding the project to a halt.

Feeling very subversive, Angela waited a few moments before she slipped from the ladies room and hurried toward the front portico where she knew Rob was waiting.

"Hi! Ready to lay the battle plan?" Rob was as crisp and fresh as ever, his well-worn suit immaculately pressed. The shoes, which Angela knew to be full of holes, were polished to a high gloss.

"Battle plan?" The odd choice of words pulled Angela from her visual journey across Rob's broad shoulders and slim waist to the impish grin on his face.

"Sure. Strategy. Plotting to keep your young client from hanging himself and you with him."

"Rob, if you'd just drop this suit . . ."

"But I won't and you know it. What I *will* do is help you with the boy. There's no sense losing a good kid, no matter what his father is like."

"I'm not so sure Kevin *is* a 'good kid,' Rob. Not any more. He's been in trouble so many times that—"

"No one is a lost cause, Angie. Come on, let's talk over lunch." Rob stretched out a hand to catch her slim one, but she pulled away sharply, still cognizant of the fears that had haunted her lately.

"And another thing! *Don't* call me Angie! It's Angela. Angie is so, so . . . unprofessional!"

Undaunted, Rob captured the resisting hand and leaned near her ear. "I'll save it for our more . . . private moments. Is that all right?" His lips brushed her ear and the silky wave of her hair whispered against her neck. Angela gave a blissful shudder before she turned on him, an empty, protective gaze masking her features.

"And who says we'll have any 'private moments?' Aren't you being rather presumptuous, *Mr*. Jordan?" Rob could stir her emotions too rapidly. He needed to be kept at bay.

Undismayed, Rob traced a meandering line with his

finger beginning at the diamond stud in her ear lobe and ending near her collarbone. "I don't believe a word of it, *Miss* Malone. I felt that electricity spark every bit as much as you!"

Suddenly realizing that they were stopped midstream in lunch hour traffic, forcing passersby to divide on either side of them like a sand bar in a river, Angela grabbed Rob's hand from her shoulder and pulled him into the nearest café.

Shrouded in darkness, they both began blinking rapidly, making the adjustment from bright noonday sun to the encompassing blackness of the restaurant.

"May I show you a table?" The maître d' intoned over their shoulders causing them to spin in unison to face him.

"I suppose so, now that we're here." Rob's voice was not happy in the slowly lifting darkness.

Berating herself for dragging him into a restaurant she knew full well he could not afford, Angela bit her lower lip in disgust. She had never known what it was to be penniless. It was vastly irritating to enjoy someone so much when he was so hopelessly low on the social ladder.

Angela's analytical mind tabulated quickly the differences between them. Her penthouse apartment versus his seedy, college town address; her designer clothing and his worn suits; her furs, her jewels, her artwork, her sports car, his . . . Volkswagen.

"Let's get out of here." Angela slipped out of Rob's casual embrace and slid around the horseshoe bench to free herself from the table.

"Already? What about lunch?"

"Let's compromise and go to the cafeteria near my office. It should be halfway between heavy French cuisine and a hot-dog stand." Angela grinned.

"Sold! You'll get used to hanging around with me yet, Angela. You've become too accustomed to the finer things in life. I had to learn how to make do with caviar taste and a beans budget!"

"That's the very thing I can't understand, Rob. You gave up a high-paying, prestigious job to give away your services in the most depressing slum in Illinois. Now you pinch pennies and take on hopeless cases on contingent fees. It just doesn't make sense!" Her voice crescendoed as they passed the maître d'.

"As a Christian, this is where I can best serve God and my fellow man. And anyway, if I had any money, I'd probably just spend it—or give it away." Rob glanced sideways at her, licking his lower lip with the tip of his tongue and then grabbing the lip in his teeth. Arching his eyebrows and cocking his head to one side, he appealed to Angela with his eyes.

"Please, Rob!" she whispered and glanced furtively around. "Must you talk about this Christian stuff so loudly?"

But she had lost her audience, for as her eyes turned back to Rob, she found him digging deep into the pockets of his suit for coins that he promptly tossed into the cup of a blind man playing an accordion on the curb.

"Bless you. Thank you. Bless you." The man intoned as the silver clattered into his cup.

Before she realized what was happening, Rob had reached over to pat the man on the shoulder. Grabbing Rob by his suit tails, Angela pulled him upright and maneuvered him to the middle of the pavement, losing themselves in the crowd.

"Whatever were you doing that for?" she hissed through clenched teeth.

"Because he's a good musician. Don't you agree?"

"Rob!" The exasperation in her voice mounted. "If you can't afford coffee in a fine French restaurant, you certainly can't afford to be throwing money away in some beggar's cup!"

"Oh, I can afford it, Angie. We just disagree on how I chose to spend it!"

"Well, what about that saying: 'God helps those

who help themselves?' Where does that fit into your theology?''

Chuckling, Rob replied, ''I think that's a quote from Benjamin Franklin, Angela, not the Bible. But it was a good try!''

Embarrassed, she tried another approach. ''Don't you ever worry about not having enough to live on?''

''Not really. I always think of the widow of Zarephath. She had only enough grain and oil for one meal. After that, she knew she and her son would starve to death. Elijah, a total stranger, came along and asked her to share their last, pitiful, meal with him. You can be sure she didn't like it one bit. But, miraculously, that batch of meal and oil never ran out. It fed the three of them for the duration of a famine. I think that I can learn a lesson from that, Angie. Sometimes God has to ask us to give of ourselves for our own good. And it's not the size of the gift, but its quality.''

''But Rob, . . . you keep giving away the money you need to spend on your own meals!''

''A poor person giving all the pennies he has gives a greater gift than the rich person who gives without sacrifice. It's like it says in Luke 21:4, about contributing out of abundance or out of poverty. Which is the greater gift?''

Angela knew she couldn't argue. She could even see a grain of sense in his words. But she still didn't want to be humiliated in public by his displays.

''Well, try not to be so banner-waving, militantly Christian around *me*. It's embarrassing. What if one of my friends had come along while I was pulling you away from there?''

''You should have left my coat tails alone, Angie. It seems to me that *you* were making the scene, not me.'' Again Rob grinned, leaving Angela more frustrated than ever.

After lunch, Angela rolled over in her mind the

nebulous thoughts she had been having about Rob as they walked toward her office. His attitude was unfathomable. He seemed to be happily penniless when he could be pulling down a huge salary at a rival firm across town.

The figures had been mentioned when her co-workers discovered who was representing Hannah Green. Rob's reputation was flawless but it was incomprehensible to all how a young man with such promise could step from an income in the five-figure range to one that probably did not adequately cover basic expenses.

She would watch and wait, observing Rob Jordan carefully, waiting for him to waiver. That aura of sweetness and love would diminish. And Angela was curious to know what would happen when it did.

As they neared Angela's office, they could hear the thud of flesh against flesh and the jeers and catcalls of a street fight. Rob turned into the alley and muttered under his breath.

Three boys were hammering on a fourth whose legs jerked off the concrete with each pounding blow to his midsection.

"Rob! That's Kevin!" Angela gasped, recognizing the frightened, bloodied face of her young client.

Rob ran, yelling, toward the silk-jacketed trio. The three, not willing to take on the furious colossus barreling toward them, took off, after one final, painful kick to Kevin's abdomen.

Rob pulled the boy to his feet as Angela neared the pair.

"Stay out of my life!" Kevin spat. "I don't need any more of my dad's hired help baby-sitting me! Especially some uptight chick and her stupid boy-friend."

"Just a minute, young man," Angela interrupted. "Three more minutes in that street brawl and the police would have been the ones pulling you out!"

"So why didn't you let them? It means a bigger fee for you, doesn't it? More court appearances? More bucks?" Kevin wiped a trickle of blood across his face, making his appearance more pitiful than before. His torn shirt hung from one shoulder and his Swiss wristwatch lay shattered on the street.

"Actually, I *am* wondering why we didn't leave him, Angie. Wouldn't it have been easier to let him get himself splattered all over the pavement and be done with it?" Rob spoke from the side of a graffiti-scrawled building where he had leaned, chewing casually on a toothpick.

Angela and Kevin spun to face him, their jaws both slack with amazement.

"And another thing, Mr. Hotshot Simmons, I'm not on your dad's payroll. If I choose to pull you out of some street squabble, I have my own reasons." The challenging tone did not go unnoticed.

"Oh, yeah? What reasons? Name one!" Kevin's fists clenched and unclenched at his sides. The young jaw squared, hiding the quiver that threatened.

Angela's eyes grew round. This was a side of Rob she had never seen before.

"All right. I can't stand to see anyone—even you—waste his life brawling in the streets with thugs, vandalizing property or turning into a petty thief. You've got promise, Kev, and I can't stand to see you waste it." Rob's tone had softened now that he had the boy's undivided attention, and he unfolded himself from the pseudo-relaxed stance he had taken. Putting out one hand, he took the boy by the shoulder.

"Come on. My apartment is closer than Angela's. Let's go there. We'll clean you up and take you home. *If* you agree to my suggestions, that is."

"What suggestions? I don't have to listen to you! You aren't my attorney. *She* is!" Kevin pointed a grubby finger toward Angela who was following the small procession, bewildered by the sudden turn of events.

Kevin had been their topic of conversation as they turned onto the street near her office. She had had word that the boy had grown wilder and more incorrigible in recent days, and Angela was terrified that his behavior would land them both in trouble from which they couldn't extricate themselves. She was bemoaning her situation to Rob, when they had come upon the street fight.

Grateful that her appointment calendar was open for the rest of the day, she decided to watch and wait to see how Rob would resolve this predicament.

"Too bad, kid. I pulled you out of the fight. Now you owe me the courtesy of listening to me. But, first, I want you to wash your face."

Using Angela's Mercedes, they quickly reached Rob's apartment. Music blared from the roof where a group of the residents were sunbathing. Kevin's eyes lighted with interest at the college students milling about, then narrowed and darted suspiciously between Rob and Angela.

"Quit dragging your feet, and get in here," Rob ordered as they reached the apartment. The tiny procession made its way into the dim recesses of the apartment.

"Rob! Your furniture! It's gone!" Angela gasped as they entered the vast, hollow room.

"I warned you. Mom is doing a contemporary condominium and remembered the things she had loaned me. She wasn't very happy that I'd broken the base for those futon mattresses. She took the two whole ones and left me the broken one to fix."

Stripped of the lovely furniture, the apartment had a whole new feel. Angela saw for the first time the peeling paint and chipped windowsills. Uncovered now, she could see the worn flooring. Amazed that she could have missed the poverty of the room at her first visit, she gazed about in wonder. How had she become so distracted by things—all that on-loan-but-elegant furniture—that she missed what was underneath? Rob had said the furniture wasn't his. Hadn't she wanted to believe that?

Now curious about this elusive mother of Rob's, Angela turned to question him, but he was gone and she could hear voices drifting from the bathroom.

"Ow! That hurts!" Kevin yelped.

"You asked for it, buddy. Now take it like a man."

Rob was applying antiseptic to Kevin's face and the boy jumped with every touch. Rob's tone was gruff, but Angela, meandering into the bathroom, noticed how gentle his hands were and how Kevin's defensive posture had diminished under Rob's attention.

She posed the question that had been grating on her mind. "So, fellows, what do we do next?"

Kevin started slightly from his position on the antiquated hourglass shaped stool and Rob shifted against the clawfooted, chipped enamel bathtub on which he was resting his weight.

"What do you mean?" Kevin asked suspiciously. "Why are you two hanging around me anyway? Nobody else does."

"To keep you out of trouble. Don't you remember anything the judge told you?"

"No. Wasn't listening, but . . . hey! That's where I remember you from! You were the guy who bumped into Miss Malone at the courthouse!" Kevin forgot his injuries as he put the puzzle pieces in place. "You were pushing some little old lady in a wheelchair. I remember now. . . ."

"Good job, Einstein, you remembered. Now don't try to get us off the track. We still have to figure out how to make you behave," Rob interjected.

"What's the diff, mister? Think it's going to be an 'in' with the lady lawyer?" The boy sneered.

"There have got to be easier ways to get an 'in,' as you call it, than trying to be *your* pal." Rob cheerfully countered, slathering antiseptic on the boy's scraped shoulder. "I've met porcupines and cacti that I'd rather cuddle up to than you. But you're more special than you think, and I'd like you to realize it."

Kevin stared, mouth gaping, at the big blond man before him pulling sterile gauze from a cardboard box. The boy's eyes followed Rob's gentle hands as they laid the gauze across his shoulder.

"Why'd you say that?"

"Why did I say what?" Rob countered as he applied white tape from a roll to the edges of the bandage.

"That I was special. You said I was special. Nobody's ever said I was special before. What's your angle?"

"No angle. You just are. We're all special, Kev. God made us that way. One of a kind. Unique. Special."

"What does God have to do with all of this? You aren't going to turn preacher on me, are ya?" Kevin's eyes had narrowed to suspicious slits. Angela held her breath, waiting for Rob's response, knowing how important it could be.

"Not today, pal. Someday, maybe. When you're ready. But till you are, I'll talk like you do—tough and mean. And I won't mean it any more than you do." Rob grinned and tousled the boy's dark hair with a free hand. Then, pulling Kevin to his feet, he led him past Angela into the barren living room.

"Want something to eat before we take you home? I've got ice cream, canned peaches, tuna. . ."

"Home!" Kevin wailed. "I don't want to go home!"

"You have to, Kevin," Angela said. "You can't spend your nights on the streets. Remember what the judge said. . . ."

"But I'll pick you up after work tomorrow and we can go shoot a few baskets—*if* your mother or the maid tells me you've been home all day." Rob threw out the offer as if it were the most natural thing in the world for him and the errant Kevin to spend an afternoon together." Then he added, "That is, if you can even *play* basketball."

"Play ball? Me? You bet I can! When was the last time you set foot on a court?" Kevin thrust out his jaw defiantly.

"I'll never tell. Just be ready at five tomorrow night. What's your address?"

"Rob! You can't trot over there and pick him up!" Angela interrupted, giving Rob a meaningful stare. "Are you sure that's wise?"

"Would your parents object to something as innocent as a basketball game?"

"My dad would object to *anything*," Kevin put in, a hint of disappointment crossing his features.

"Then Miss Malone will pick you up. I'll meet you at the court. Wear your tennis shoes, Angie." Before she could reply, Rob had wrapped Kevin in one of his own shirts and hustled him out the door to a taxi cab.

Rob returned shortly to Angela, who had her arms crossed over her chest and was tapping one leather-shod toe against the marred wooden floor.

"And just what do you think you're doing? Who says I will pick up that . . . delinquent . . . and take him somewhere to play basketball with you, another overgrown kid?"

"It's part of the plan. Don't you remember?"

"Plan—what plan?"

"To keep Kevin out of mischief while I'm suing his father for Hannah Green! I've told you before, I won't drop my case, but I will help you try to salvage Kevin. He's a good kid, Angie. It's a shame to see him waste his life." Rob spread the single remaining futon on the floor as he spoke and sank down upon it wearily.

Regret flooded over Angela as she realized how much kindness and generosity Rob had shown today—and she had not even appreciated it.

Sinking down next to him, she put a tentative hand on his shoulder. "I'm sorry, Rob. I didn't think. You do care about Kevin, don't you? And you even mean what you told him."

"Every word of it. You've read that poster that stores are selling nowadays—'I'm special. God doesn't make junk.' I believe it completely. And Kevin just reminded me again."

"Then why all the tough talk, Rob? You sounded almost mean!"

"It's what he understands right now. We have to reach him where he is. We have to let him know we care, but in a language he can understand. I'm involved with a project similar to the Big Brother program, and I've been forced to think about this a lot. I've had some very troubled boys as my little brothers. So far, the approach has worked." Rob ran long fingers through his sandy hair with obvious weariness. He leaned his head against the wall and closed his eyes.

Studying his chiseled profile, Angela's heart began to thump harder within her chest. He was a mystery all right, giving more of himself than he actually had to give. She read in Rob's weariness the frustration of not enough time or money to do all he wanted to do. She and Kevin were obviously but one tiny aspect of his life, but the more she knew of Rob Jordan, the more she wanted to know.

Warning bells rang in her brain and Angela forced herself off the mattress to begin pacing the empty floor.

*What's the matter with me?* she chided herself. Rob Jordan was nothing more than a path to poverty. Where were all those lofty, diamond-encrusted goals she had set for herself? Whatever possessed her to be attracted to this obvious loser? *It must be physical*, she decided, eyeing the long expanse of man as he sleepily stretched out before her.

Her dark eyes followed the attractive curve of his shoulder down to the strong, muscular chest and trim waistline and paused a moment over the lean, hard line of his thighs. Whatever the reason for the attraction, it was there, making Angela Malone quail at the impact it was having on her senses.

Her eyes made the journey upward again only to be met by amused blue eyes.

"What's on your mind? Some serious thoughts?"

Angela flushed involuntarily and as the rosy pinkness bled across her cheeks, Rob's eyebrow arched in surprise.

Before he could speak and rattle her further, she gathered up her purse and headed for the door.

"Don't forget about basketball," he called after her. "I'll be on the courts two blocks south of here. And be on time!"

Angela turned sharply to retort, but Rob had already readjusted his position, curled one arm under his head and closed his eyes.

Smiling in spite of herself, Angela shut the door quietly and slipped out.


"Shoot, Angie! Don't just stand there! Shoot!"

Angela Malone, named to the city's list of best-dressed professional women, cited as the current outstanding female member of one of Chicago's legal organizations, and frequent inhabitant of Mr. Marc's chair at the fashionable and trendy Hair Academy, was standing disconsolately in baggy gray sweats and outrageously expensive New Balance tennis shoes. Her inclination was to drop the ball and cover her ears as Rob and Kevin clamored for her to shoot the basketball in her hands.

Finally, she closed her eyes, slammed the ball into the concrete and stomped off the court. "Quit yelling at me! Is that all basketball is, yelling?"

Instantaneously, Rob and Kevin were at her side, apologizing and cajoling her to return to the game.

"Come on, Angie! We were just trying to help you. We weren't yelling at you!" Rob pleaded, laughter barely concealed in his voice.

"You were so! This is a disgusting game!" She sank onto a grassy knoll and her two playmates tumbled after her.

"You didn't think it was so disgusting when you made that basket! I think this is good for you. It's taking some of the starch out of you. You need to unbend."

"Unbend! Unbend! Why, I'll have you know I'm the most flexible person in my office!"

"Well, that doesn't say much!" Rob hooted as Angela came diving toward him, pummeling his chest.

"Now who's yelling?" Kevin interjected, grinning at the two rolling on the ground next to him. Suddenly serious, he added, more to himself than the others, "Anyway, you don't know what yelling is until you've been yelled at by my dad."

Angela and Rob exchanged potent looks and ended their playful interlude, both studying the now quiet boy from their cross-legged positions on the grass.

"Want to talk about it?" Rob queried nonchalantly.

"What's to talk about? Miss Malone has heard him blow up. And when he yells, he *means* it!" Angela could see Kevin wither at the thought.

"Did he yell at you today, Kevin?" Angela asked softly.

"Yeah, but I guess it was my fault. I stayed out of the way most of the day, but when I thought he had gone to work I came downstairs and there he was."

"So what did he yell about?" Rob stretched out catlike, resting his sandy blond head on the grass.

"He could tell that I'd been fighting by all the scrapes on my face. Said he'd fire Miss Malone and just let me go to jail and rot. But I think he was mad about something else, because almost as soon as he said it, he seemed to forget I was there. I just took off." The boy shrugged lightly, dispelling the mood.

Angela and Rob glanced at each other, the look fraught with meaning. Milton Simmons was furious all right, but it had nothing to do with Kevin. He was only an object on which to vent frustration.

"Whoa! It's nearly seven! I gotta go! I promised that I'd be home for dinner." Kevin leapt to his feet in one fluid motion. Turning to the two still sitting on the grass, he smiled and said. "Hey, thanks! Can we do it again sometime?"

Rob's gaze met the eager look in the boy's eyes. "Sure. You've got my number. Give me a call."

"Deal!" With that Kevin jogged off, looking less burdened and happier than Angela could ever remember seeing him.

"Rob, you've got to drop it." Turning to her companion, Angela gazed on the serene face, chin tilted upward, reaching for the fading sun.

"You mean the Simmons suit? You know I can't." Rob stretched lazily, belying the tension Angela could read about his mouth.

"But what about Kevin? Even he has been suffering because of his father's rages."

"Kevin was suffering long before this case came up, Angela. I'm doing him more good as a friend who will play basketball than I would if I turned back on the case. And what about Hannah Green?"

"What about her? Find her a nursing home somewhere! That's where she belongs."

"There are others, Angela, just as disenfranchised as Hannah, that Simmons has kicked out onto the street. I'd go ahead with this even without Hannah."

"There's nothing in it for you, Rob! No money, no glory, nothing."

"I'm not after money or glory, Angie. You know that. This is my duty, my calling, if you will. Remember Corinthians—"

"I know, I know. All that stuff about those who aren't strong or powerful or nobly born being chosen by God to shame the wise, but . . ." she looked hopeful, "maybe that doesn't apply here."

Rob rolled onto his side and their gazes locked. "It applies more than ever here, Angie. Don't try to convince me otherwise."

A freshet of unreasonable anger raged through her then. Why couldn't he understand? He was everything that she didn't want in a man—and everything that she did. He embarrassed and frustrated her at every turn, giving his jacket to a cold child when he needed it to get into the theater with her, handing out money to his clients and ending up with only enough to eat at a roadside stand, promising to meet her only to call and say he was needed at the hospital or jail.

She had not counted on falling in love, especially with a man who seemed to love everyone else more than he could ever love her. Tears threatened to fall as Angela spun away.

Turning back angrily, she vented her frustration and dismay, "Then keep Hannah Green and all your other pitiful clients! But don't call me. I'm not another act of charity, Rob. Goodbye."

From the corner of her eye, she could see Kevin. He'd come back for his jacket. How much of their conversation had he overheard? None, she hoped. She didn't need that right now.

Angela stumbled toward the edge of the park, unaccustomed to the thick-soled tennis shoes. Secretly hoping to hear the light tread of Rob's footsteps behind her, she cast a furtive glance over her shoulder as she reached the street, but Rob had taken her at her word. She was alone.

## CHAPTER 5

ANOTHER SATURDAY. Angela glared at the hands of her bedside clock. She trudged into the sleek black and silver bathroom to stare into the mirror. Dark eyes resting in muddy pools stared back at her.

*I never expected him to do what I asked! Just because I said not to call—I didn't mean it!*

Slapping cold water onto her cheeks, Angela followed the mechanical routine that prepared her for the day.

Relief flooded through her at the sound of the telephone.

"Hello."

"Hello, Angela, it's Jennifer. Are you awake?"

"Oh, hi, Jenna. Barely. What's up?"

"I was watching you at work yesterday. You need a change of pace. And I decided to apply my world-famous, ultimate cure-all for a case of the blues—a shopping spree. How does that sound?"

Angela smiled crookedly at the receiver. Her façade of cheerfulness was obviously not holding up. But, then, Jennifer would always be the first to notice.

"It sounds wonderful, Jenna. I *have* been a little . . . down . . . lately. A good, old-fashioned, cathartic day of spending might be just what I need!"

"My thoughts exactly. I'll pick you up in front of your building at ten sharp. See ya!" Jennifer Brady's chipper voice disappeared with a click and Angela stared into the receiver, willing it to spring to life again, only this time with Rob Jordan's lazy drawl.

Suddenly furious with her uncharacteristic moping, she rammed the receiver into its cradle and railed at the enveloping walls. "Well, then *don't* call, you big lug! See if I care!" Slamming into her immense walk-in closet, Angela began to pull clothing from the padded hangers marching in meticulous rows all around her.

Still muttering, she tugged a black cotton jumpsuit across her slim hips and lassoed a shell and rope belt around her waist. Flipping the back of the collar upward at a jaunty angle and slipping her feet into backless black suede slides, she then dared the full-length mirror before her to reflect the ravages of Rob Jordan's absence from her life.

"Rob Jordan, you self-righteous, pompous, know-it-all, I'd like to get my hands on your throat for just two minutes. . . ." The tirade fizzled as Angela realized that given just two minutes with her hands on Rob's tanned and thickly corded neck, she would melt into his arms, the killer instinct she was nurturing turned into something far more heady and alluring.

Swinging into movement, Angela scooped a rope-and-shell shoulder bag from a bedroom chair and headed for the door. Jennifer was always early.

Just as Angela suspected, her bright blue convertible was parked next to the curb. Morning sun reflected from Jenna's pale blond hair as she bent studiously over the fingernail she was buffing.

"I thought you had a manicurist for things like that, kiddo!" Angela threw her bag into the back seat and, without opening the door, jumped onto the side of the car and swung her legs over, sliding down into the baby blue cushions.

"I do, but she's even more snobbish than I am—*she* won't work on Saturdays!" Jennifer tossed the buffer into her vast purse and slipped the purring car into gear, pulling out into the sparse morning traffic. "At least we can beat the afternoon shoppers. Where do you want to go first?"

"It doesn't matter to me. What are we buying?" Angela spoke disinterestedly, her head resting on the back of the seat and her face turned into the sun.

"Clothes! Jewels! Furs! Whatever it takes!"

"Takes for what, Jenna? What are you babbling about?" Finally, Angela sat up and peered at her friend through the inky hair whipping across her face.

"Whatever it takes to get you out of the doldrums that you've been in for the past three weeks. I've never seen you quite like this, Angela, and I've known you since law school. Nothing ever seemed to stump you. Angela Malone, perfect student, perfect lawyer. Always with an eye toward the top. You've never let day-to-day stresses get you down. *So what's going on with you now?*"

Angela groaned as she threw her head back against the car seat, squeezing her eyes shut, blocking the spectre of Rob's face. "Men, Jenna. Man, rather. One crummy, poverty-stricken, no-count man has me acting like a sixteen-year-old ingenue! Can you believe it? How embarrassing!"

"Believe it? Of me, yes. Of you, no! Angela! What happened to that game plan of yours—using men as the stepping stones to success, and when you reach the top, marry the last step! I remember the plan well."

"I know, I know. I can't figure myself out. I don't love him . . . at least, I don't think I do . . . but I can't figure him out, either. He arouses some kind of *need* in me."

That statement was met with a lecherous grin, and Angela playfully slapped at her leering companion. But Jenna would not be quieted. "A *need*, huh? Well, that explains it! It's plainly physical! We'll just find someone else to fill that need—a stepping stone, so to speak!"

"Be quiet and drive, Brady. I hear a clothing department calling me." Angela effectively distracted her friend from the playful banter, but her own words clattered in her head like castanets. *He arouses some kind of need in me. . . . Physical? Perhaps.* She pondered the question. *But it's more than that . . . almost, well, spiritual.* Whatever Rob Jordan had that gave him all that peace in the midst of his poverty was what she craved. He was sated, full of tranquility and joy. And she was hungry, clawing her way to the top hoping for fulfillment there.

Frightened by the serious twist her mind had taken and more alarmed still by the urgent desires that Rob aroused in her and the dearth of knowledge she held about his beliefs, Angela did what seemed to her the most logical thing. She submerged her thoughts in a heady day of extravagant spending, gamboling through Chicago's finest stores, making purchases like there was no tomorrow.

At day's end Angela strolled through the mall toward Jenna's car, boxes suspended from the fingertips of both hands. Turning into the hallway near which Jenna had parked, Angela spied a window display of contemporary furniture. The sight was as physical as a slap in the face. Before her was a replica of the pieces she had so admired in Rob's apartment.

Slowing her step to a snail's pace, Angela began to idly wonder if Rob had obtained any new pieces for his shabby apartment. Startled, she heard herself laugh. The day had come full circle—Rob was at the top of her thoughts once again.

She hurried to Jennifer's car, fuming inwardly that

Rob Jordan could have so much influence over her. She had shown him! She had spent a whole day and hardly thought of him at all—but it had cost her two months of paychecks to do it. There had to be an easier way to get Rob Jordan out of her mind!

It was Jennifer who offered a solution.

"How about a double date tonight, Angela? Or are you all worn out from shopping?"

"A *double date?* Really, Jenna! How quaint!"

"Quaint, schmaint! Brad and some friend from work are taking me out for dinner. Brad asked me to get this guy a date, but I refused because I couldn't think of a likely candidate. But here you are! Interested?"

Angela recoiled at the thought of a blind date—especially with a friend of Jennifer's engineer fiancé. Brad was pleasant but tediously boring. Any friend of his had marks against him from the start.

"Thanks, but no thanks. I don't want to spend an evening learning about the stress factors of suspension bridges. I've done that before with Brad's friends. Have fun without me!" Angela wearily climbed out of the convertible, using the door this time. Her Olympian shopping day was finally telling in her tired step. It had succeeded in wiping away her energy, if not her errant thoughts of Rob.

Trudging down the length of hall toward her apartment, Angela felt an overwhelming surge of loneliness. Supper smells wafted from several apartments, teasing her nostrils with the cozy hint of roast beef and warm gravy.

Inside her own apartment the atmosphere had a glacial quality—everything was cold, immaculate, pristine—and, in her present mood, uninviting. Suddenly unable to bear the thought of an evening alone, Angela dropped the armload of packages and headed for the phone.

She listened to the ring nearly twenty times before a breathless Jenna came on the line.

70

"Hello? Hello? Are you still there?"

"I'm here. It's Angela."

"Angela! I just left you! What did you do, wave goodbye and then dial my number?"

"Just about. I've changed my mind. I'll go with you and Brad tonight."

"Great! After dinner the four of us can go dancing, and then—"

"Hold it, friend. I'll go out for dinner. This is not a blind date you're foisting on me. I just want company tonight, amusing company, to get my mind off—things."

"'Things', huh? Well according to Brad, his friend Mike should be just the answer. We'll pick you up at eight."

Eight o'clock arrived all too quickly. Angela was still putting the polishing touches on her sleek page-boy when the doorbell chimed. She glided through the room on silver slippers, the glinting metallic thread that ran through the woven knit of her gray dress dancing in the muted light.

She flung open the apartment door, ready to greet the familiar forms of Jennifer and Brad. Instead, before her was a slight, dark-haired man groomed to a painful gloss in a black suit and white shirt, his hands primly folded across his midriff. When the door was fully opened, he carefully uncoiled one manicured hand and extended it toward Angela.

"Miss Malone? I'm Michael Renfrow, a friend of Brad and Jennifer." After that statement Mr. Renfrow's slightly worried expression settled into prudish contentment, and he waited for Angela's response.

Wildly, Angela thought of a small but distinguished penguin, and wondered if anyone had ever mistakenly called him Wilbur. It seemed so much more fitting a name for the man than Mike. Michael was a name like Rob's, strong and masculine, to be worn only by those who could meet its challenge.

Disturbed that Rob could worm his way into her thoughts by such a perverse path, Angela flung her arm expansively toward the center of the apartment and greeted Michael Renfrow with much more warmth than she actually felt.

"So nice to meet you! Come in. I'll get my wrap and we can go. Where are Brad and Jennifer?" Whipping a cashmere shawl from the chair, she hid her face, afraid the mutinous thoughts she was harboring would be reflected in her features.

*You must be insane, Angela Malone! How could a man like this make me forget Rob?*

"Shall we go?" Turning to face her escort, Angela arranged a composed expression. She had asked Rob not to call. And she had gotten herself into this date. There was no place to go but forward.

Angela rolled over one more time in her sleepy, silken dream and was jarred awake by the distressing sensation of hanging over the edge of a cliff, suspended over a deep crevasse, in imminent danger of falling. Her head jerked back sharply as she discovered she was millimeters from tumbling out of bed.

"My goodness, I slept soundly last night!" she muttered aloud as she rolled back toward the middle of the bed, stretching and curling like a tabby in a sunlit window, snuggling deep into the pillowy satin comforter in which she was tangled.

Last night. The memories came avalanching over her and a groan escaped her lips. Michael Renfrow and the stress factors! It had been worse than she had imagined. At every turn she found herself comparing him with Rob—and he came up sadly lacking.

Rob. That poverty-stricken, religion-espousing, shabbily dressed man had the ability to sink her into a quagmire of the doldrums with his absence.

Padding from the bedroom into the tiny efficiency kitchen, Angela tossed a handful of coffee beans into the grinder and whizzed them into a coarse powder. She measured the powder into the basket of her coffeepot and filled the chrome contraption with icy tap water. As the potion brewed, she popped a frozen croissant into the toaster oven. She couldn't remember the last time she had heated the range oven. One baked potato or a four-ounce portion of fish looked so pitifully out of place in the cavern of the stove, that she had purchased the countertop version. Her food looked less lonely heating in the smaller confines.

Toes cool from the kitchen tile, Angela foraged around for the turquoise slippers that matched her bright silk pajamas. With one ear tuned to the still gurgling coffeepot, Angela flipped on the small color TV on the counter between the kitchen and dining area of the apartment.

Onto the screen flickered a rotund figure decked out in Sunday finery. Even without the sound, Angela could guess the message of the evangelist clutching the edge of the pulpit in fervent emotion.

"Oh, Rob, how can you stand that stuff!" she thought aloud. Wrinkling her nose in distaste, she flicked off the switch. Nothing but sermons and overly dramatized programs meant to take watchers on guilt trips on Sunday mornings, reminding them of the hungry, the aged, the lonely. "I've got enough trouble of my own without watching that rubbish!"

Just then, the coffeepot burbled and a tiny ding signaled that the croissant was warm. Carrying her sparse breakfast to the table on a lacquered tray, Angela set a place setting with a linen napkin and a crystal glass of strawberry preserves. She rearranged the butter dish and jam twice, before the dishes seemed aligned. The thought drifted into her consciousness that she was avoiding sitting down to that lonely meal.

"I'll read, . . . that's what I'll do," Angela decided aloud and headed for the low-slung bookcase that encompassed the perimeters of the room. Her hand fell on a black cowhide covered volume, and she pulled it from its niche. Gold embossed letters glittered up at her—HOLY BIBLE.

"Oh, no!" she moaned. What was it about Sunday mornings? Couldn't you get away from religion *anywhere?* Succumbing to what seemed to be overwhelming odds against her, Angela took the book to the table and began to thumb through it as she ate.

Her pleasure mounted as she found in her grandmother's spidery scrawl the birth and death history of the Malone family, recorded on parchment pages inside the leather volume. Her coffee cooled and the croissant was forgotten as Angela flipped through the nearly translucent pages of the old Bible. *Genesis. Psalms. Proverbs.* Familiar words, yet foreign. *Matthew. Luke. Romans. Corinthians.*

*Corinthians! Rob's chapter! What had he said? Was it First or Second Corinthians? Why did they have two, anyway? Surely one Corinthians would have been enough!* Angela's hands flew through the pages, thumbing purposefully.

It *was* here! The words leapt out at her from the page: "Consider your call, brethren, not many of you were wise . . . not many were powerful, not many were of noble birth; but God chose what is foolish in the world to shame the wise, God chose what is weak . . . to shame the strong . . . so that no human being might boast in the presence of God. . . . Let him who boasts, boast of the Lord."

The memories of the evening before bore down upon her. Michael's crowing, preening, egotistical, pretentious ways had worn on her sensibilities until she wanted to scream. His obvious wealth and position could not outweigh his arrogant, swaggering, high-hatted ways. By comparison, Rob's humble demeanor and self-effacing humor seemed as refreshing as an oasis in the desert.

She had read Rob wrong. She assumed he was like all the other men she had known. Another man might have disregarded her request for solitude, but Rob had not. And now she was paying the price. In fact, she was finding that it was an exacting fee.

Angela skimmed the pages of her grandmother's Bible. Passages and verses caught her attention, familiar words that she had heard reached out at her, showing her for the very first time their origin. Intrigued, she pushed aside her cup and plate, curled her feet under her hips on the cushiony leather chair and read.

Nearly an hour had passed when the disruptive jangle of the telephone jarred her from her study.

"Hello?" Angela spoke shortly, irritated by the intrusion.

"Miss Malone? Is this Miss Angela Malone?"

"Speaking. Who is calling please?"

"This is the Chicago Police Department. We are holding a young man who says he's your client. The name is Kevin Simmons. He would like to speak with you."

Angela's heart sank. Kevin! In jail! That spelled disaster for both of them.

"I'll be right down, officer. Tell Kevin I'm coming." Slamming the receiver back into its cradle, Angela whirled around once in a controlled frenzy before turning back to the phone. Her years of training seemed to fly out the window. This time her *own* career was in jeopardy as well as her client's. She needed advice.

"Rob! I'll have to call Rob. He'll know what to do." Her nervous fingers nearly quivered from the numbered slots as she dialed. She had just decided to give up after several rings when a breathless voice came on the line.

"Yeah! Hi! Are you still there?"

"Rob! It's Angela."

75

"Angela! Well, this is a surprise. Sorry I took so long to answer. I was outside in the hall trying to fit my key into the lock. Do you know that it rang—"

"Eighteen times before you answered? Yes, I know, I counted. Rob, I may need your help. We're in trouble. Well, *I'm* in trouble. No, not exactly. It's *Kevin*."

"Kevin? Now what's happening? I haven't seen him since . . . since that day in the park."

Angela's heart sank. She had affected more than herself with her impulsive behavior.

"He's in jail. The police just called. I suppose he wants his attorney. This is the end of it for both Kevin and me. Milton Simmons will have both of us out on our ears as soon as he gets wind of this." Her voice wavered and silence hovered on the line for a moment. Then Rob broke in.

"I'll meet you at the jail. How long will it take you to get there?"

A sigh of relief shuddered through Angela and she closed her eyes for a blissful second. He was still willing to help her! Then, businesslike, she eyed her watch. "Give me thirty minutes. I'm not dressed yet."

"Okay. I just got home from church, so I'm ready. But I have a longer drive. See you then. 'Bye."

Angela hugged the receiver for a brief moment before setting it gently into its cradle. Then, springing into action, she bolted into her bedroom.

Thirty minutes later she stepped onto the sidewalk in front of the police station. Her appearance belied the frantic haste with which she had dressed. A navy cable-knit sweater dress fit trimly over her slim hips. Her only bit of whimsy was a bright yellow belt and earrings flashing in the noontime sun.

A second car pulled up only seconds behind hers, this one rumbling and sputtering like a tubercular old man. The Volkswagen nudged within inches of the rear of Angela's car, and the motor died slowly with a series of burps and sputters.

Rob slammed out of the car, an apologetic expression on his face. "Wrong gas."

"What?" Of all the things Angela had imagined he might say when they met again, that was not one of them.

"Wrong type of gas. It makes the car engine stop by degrees. Sometimes it takes a full minute to settle down. Poor old thing belches like an Irishman after an Italian meal. How are you, Angie?"

Flustered by the non sequiturs, Angela hardly knew how to respond.

"Fine. . . . Okay, awful!" She was terrified at the condition in which she might find Kevin and relieved to know that Rob had come to their rescue.

"I've missed you, Angela. It's been hard not to call."

"Well, then why didn't you?" She squared off, facing him on the street, suddenly angry at his inattentiveness.

"You asked me not to—remember? But you aren't a charity case in my book, Angie. I just wanted you to know that."

"Well, let's put that in past tense, Rob. I *wasn't* a charity case. But I am now. Kevin and I are in big trouble, and I've run out of ideas. If I can't pull him out of this one without a fuss, Milton Simmons will have us both tarred and feathered and ridden out of town on a rail."

"As much as I've always wanted to see exactly how that's done, I think I'll try to prevent it this time. Let's go inside and see what young master Simmons has to say for himself."

Rob extended a tanned hand toward Angela. She could see the deeply creased lifeline on his palm, and she clutched it as if it were her own as well. Unless Rob could think of a way out of this mess, she would be out of the firm by morning, and Kevin would be on his way to juvenile detention.

A pang of regret shot through her. She should never have spent all that money on clothing. Not if she were to be jobless. And the possibility was more than likely.

A young man in a light tan suit met them just inside the door of the station house. His eyes lit as he spied Rob.

"Hi, Mr. Jordan. Working on Sunday, I see."

"As little as possible, Wilson. We seem to have a minor emergency down here."

"Anything to do with my clients?"

"Maybe. Are you familiar with a Kevin Simmons?" The young man's eyes darkened, and the easy smile faded. "More than familiar. I've been assigned to his case. Just got arrested in a gang fight."

"Then you're the man we want to see. I'd like to introduce you to Angela Malone, Kevin's attorney. Angela, this is Jerry Wilson, juvenile parole officer."

"Pleased to meet you, Mr. Wilson. Perhaps we should talk about Kevin before Rob and I go in to see him."

"I'd like you to see the boy first. He's sullen and uncooperative. Maybe you can get him to change his attitude. Otherwise, my options are limited as to what I can recommend for him."

Angela's stomach lurched at the soft words. "Options are limited" was the equivalent of more incarceration. And that meant public humiliation for the Simmons family. And Angela knew where that would lead for her—on a job hunt.

"Can you take us to him?"

"I'll get an officer to do that. I'll be waiting for you in the conference room when you're done. Good luck." The soft-spoken Mr. Wilson gave a thumbs-up sign to the pair as they followed a uniformed officer down the hallway toward the detention center.

Rob's warm hand encasing hers was her only comfort in the trek down the long gray hall of cells. Each time a barrier had to be opened, Angela eyed it carefully, shuddering when it slammed shut behind her, locking her further away from freedom. *What must Kevin be thinking right now? This was the worst mess he had gotten into so far. Would it be the last, or one of many more?*

"He'll be fine, Angie. We'll make sure of that." She could feel Rob's warm breath near her ear, and he answered her unspoken thoughts.

"Here he is. Hey, Simmons! You got company." The officer turned the key in the lock, and the door to Kevin's cell swung open. After Rob and Angela had entered, the door was pulled shut behind them with another isolating clang.

Kevin lay on the single cot, his head directly in line with the open toilet, his feet curled to his buttocks in a nearly fetal position. He looked younger than his years in the prison gray pajamas and pale in the fluorescent light radiating from the ceiling.

Slowly, in jerky stops and starts, like the transparencies of a movie film in a projector gone bad, he raised himself from the cot, facing forward, never meeting their eyes. There was a new stiffness in his movements, vastly different from the fluid, springiness of the boy playing basketball less than a month before.

Understanding dawned when he turned toward them and Angela saw the spreading bruise that meandered across the entire left side of his face and jaw. His blackened eye was nearly closed, and a jagged red tear issued out across his cheekbone. His ear was swollen and tender looking.

"Looks like you really got yourself into it this time, kid." Rob observed, seemingly unperturbed by the ugly sight.

"What's it to you?" Kevin did his best to sneer, but

79

the stiffness in his jaw prevented much more than a defiant twitch.

"Not much. It's your business if you want to get your head beaten in. It's when you want to get out of jail that it becomes *my* business."

"*She's* my lawyer. Not *you*." Kevin pointed a grubby finger at Angela who had maneuvered herself behind Rob's right shoulder.

"And she called me. Does that satisfy you?"

"I thought you two were fighting. I was there; I know. 'Don't call me. I'm not one of your charity cases.' I remember what she said. Well, I'm not one of your charity cases, either, so just get lost, Jordan. If you two can't get along, why do you expect me to get along with my old man or anyone else? I see how it works. You can't fool me."

Angela looked at Rob in dismay. That little tiff had had more far-reaching effects than she had ever imagined. She had never meant it to be an example of interpersonal relationships, but Kevin had overheard. Now the damage had to be undone.

"Kevin, I was wrong that day. I said things that I didn't mean, and I've regretted them ever since. Rob's my friend and I sent him away. You're my friend too. And I want you both back." Out of the corner of her eye, Angela caught Rob's grin, which quickly disappeared as Kevin turned an appraising eye on him.

"What's the scam?"

"Actually, I think she means it. Should we give her another chance? She's your ticket out of here, you know." Rob leaned against the concrete-block wall, arms crossed, head tilted.

"Well, this isn't the coolest place I've ever been. . . ."

"Any more stunts like this and it's going to become a permanent home. Did you ever think of that?" Rob threw out the suggestion casually.

The boy blanched and turned to Angela with an appealing look in his eyes. "I don't have to stay here now, do I? You'll take me out, won't you?"

"We'll have to talk to your parole officer. He's waiting out front."

Kevin's bravado nearly dissolved as the attending officer opened the door for Angela and Rob, and they left him huddled on the small cot. He curled his legs underneath him as they exited, resting his chin on his knees, battling threatening tears.

Back in the main receiving room of the jail, Angela began to lament: "Oh, Rob! What can we do? I feel so responsible! I should never have spoken to you in front of him the way I did. Everyone in his life fights and argues—even us!"

"It's something we'll have to settle, Angie, but right now I think that we'd better find Jerry. Tough as Kevin would like us to think he is, I'd wager he's about two minutes away from pure terror."

Nodding contritely, Angela followed him toward the conference room. Rob was doing everything she should have been doing. Where was the professional control on which she so prided herself? All her legal skills were useless unless Rob could reach Kevin. What good were all her legal wiles without Rob's ability to reach people, to touch them?

Abruptly, as it was wont to do in Rob's presence, Angela's mind changed tracks. "You're wearing a new suit!"

"Huh?"

"It's new! It's not one of the—uh—three I'm accustomed to seeing you wear." Mortified that she had blurted out her thoughts, Angela stuttered through the explanation.

Laughing and unoffended, Rob parried, "So Mom was right!"

"Mom? Right about what?"

"She insisted I get a new suit. She said everyone in

the city must be tired of the ones I'd been wearing. Obviously she was right!"

"It's very nice. Really. But I didn't mean that your others weren't. I normally don't blurt things out like that. You just seem to have that effect on me—I mean—oh, dear! I did it again, didn't I?"

This time Rob let out a deep, resonant chuckle that sprang from his diaphragm and built to a pleasant roar. And the harder he laughed, the redder Angela became.

Her violent blush reached its peak just as they burst in upon Jerry Wilson, who was studying an open file in the police-station conference room. One eyebrow surged upward in inquiry as the two entered.

Angela quickly recovered her composure under the intense scrutiny. What she and Rob accomplished in the next few minutes could decide the course of two lives—Kevin's and hers.

"Well, how did you find him?" Jerry Wilson asked, his eyes darting from Rob's large form to Angela's petite one.

"Scared stiff."

"He should be. He's in big trouble this time. Some of the gang members had weapons, and he was one of them."

Angela made a hissing sound as she drew a sharp breath. Rob muttered so only she could hear, "Blast! It's worse than I thought then."

To the man before them, Rob countered, "So what's your next step, Jerry?"

Angela steeled herself for the answer.

"Normally circumstances such as these mean automatic revocation of probation. Since Kevin received a deferred imposition of sentencing, the case should go back to the judge. If it does, the judge can sentence him in any manner he sees fit. In this case, probably a fine plus incarceration—up to thirty days."

"And a criminal record?" Rob asked, a frown furrowing his brow.

"Yes. A pretty heavy load for a young boy."

"And are you going to recommend that Kevin's case be sent back before the judge?" Angela persisted. "Or can we work something else out?" The chance was slim, but she had been a lawyer long enough to remember to explore every avenue, no matter how unlikely.

"It depends. I might be willing to supervise the remainder of Kevin's probationary period under certain circumstances." Jerry Wilson cast a telling glance toward Rob.

"Could I entice you to consider it if I offered to participate in the remainder of Kevin's period of probation?" Rob volunteered. "As you well know, I'm in the Youth Support Program. If Kevin agrees to be my little brother, will you give him another shot?" Rob had slumped into a wooden chair with a high, round back. He seemed perfectly at ease with his amazing offer.

Angela's jaw slackened, her mouth gaping in amazement. What was Rob proposing? To take on the responsibility of Milton Simmons's errant son? To attempt to salvage the son of a man who viewed Rob as the enemy? What could Rob be thinking?

## CHAPTER 6

"ROB! WHAT ARE YOU SAYING?" The words slipped out, unbidden. Shocked, Angela stared at the broad-shouldered, sandy-haired man.

"I'm saying what Jerry here expected me to say. It's our only answer. Don't you agree, Wilson?"

"Seems perfectly logical to me." Jerry Wilson turned toward the astounded Angela with a sympathetic smile. "Rob and I have worked together before, Miss Malone. He and I have attempted to salvage several troubled boys. Our success rate has been pretty good, considering. If Rob is willing to actively participate in the remainder of Kevin's probationary period, I won't refer this case to the court. Our program has been an effective tool in the past, but Kevin will also have to agree to the plan."

"Or go to juvenile detention?" she whispered.

"Probably. As I said, the options are limited." Wilson shrugged his shoulders and splayed his hands before him. He and Rob had obviously played out this scene before, but never with the son of Milton Simmons.

Simmons!

Alarm spread across Angela's face as she turned to face Rob who was fluttering the pages of a dog-eared magazine.

"Rob, what about Milt Simmons?" she hissed.

"What about him?"

"He'll never let you chaperone Kevin! He'd like *you* locked away somewhere! You're his biggest nuisance!"

"I seem to be affecting everyone that way lately," Rob said with mock sadness in his voice. "Do you think I need to change my deodorant?" He grinned impishly, biting his bottom lip with even top teeth. He was clearly unconcerned about irritating Milton Simmons, but his hand edged toward Angela's until their fingers touched.

"Be serious!" Angela cut short his hand's trek with a brusque move of her wrist, her eyes shooting daggers toward the tranquil man next to her.

"I am, Angela. Tell Kevin's father that the boy's choices are participating in a program with a court-appointed companion or having the case referred to the court for sentencing. He doesn't need to know exactly *who* the companion is, does he? The only person who seems to know anything at all about Kevin at home is the maid."

"Well, maybe." Angela wanted desperately for this approach to work, but the problems seemed insurmountable.

"If we don't do this Kevin will lose the benefit of his deferred imposition, Angela. And you know as well as I do that that means he'd have a criminal record. That's too big a burden for him to carry for the rest of his life. He's so young. I'm willing to try if you are."

Rob's blue eyes glowed with a warmth and sincerity that twisted at Angela's heart. *He really wants to do this! And for the son of Milton Simmons!* Stunned by the possibilities, Angela sat back, shaking her head, her sleek black hair gliding from side to side.

Rob Jordan was offering Kevin one more chance—and he was giving her another chance as well. Without him, both of their futures were in jeopardy.

"All right. Why not? If Mr. Wilson thinks you can do it, so do I!"

"Great!" Rob bounded from the chair. "Let's get things set up, Jerry. You can release him to Angie—uh—Angela—and she can take him home. She can be our liaison. I'll keep the kid so busy he won't have time for trouble—I hope."

The last two words were lost on Jerry Wilson who had already made for the doorway to begin the necessary procedure, but Angela skewered Rob's eyes with her own and whispered, "And what does *that* mean?"

Rob sighed, and again, Angela noticed weary lines etched around his eyes and the tired sag to his shoulders.

"My schedule has been a bit hectic lately."

"More than usual?" Angela remembered the pitiful string of clients in which Rob invested so much of himself.

"It's the paperwork that's been getting me down. That and looking for a new office to rent."

"You're moving? I thought you were happy there—hard as that is for me to believe!"

"I am happy in my present location, but ironically, it turns out that my slum lord—I mean landlord—is none other than Milton Simmons! Apparently he's been doing some research on the young upstart who's holding up construction on the project, and he discovered that, if nothing else, he could raise my rent. Gentle harassment, you might say. Unfortunately, he seems to own ninety percent of the buildings in the area. And the rest are condemned. It wouldn't matter so much, but the people there have come to depend on me!"

"That old goat! I'd like to—"

"Beat him to a pulp and break all those beautifully lacquered nails in the process? Why Angela! I didn't know you cared!" Rob was grinning again, at Angela's righteous indignation. His gentle prodding made her feel immediately how ineffective anger would be. Milton Simmons couldn't be cowed that way. There had to be another tactic.

"Then why on earth are you going to become responsible for Kevin? If Simmons is doing this to you, you don't need to be helping his son!"

"Reconciliation, Angela. That's the key word. I believe that's what God has called me to do. I'd like nothing better than to see Kevin and his father on good terms. As lawyers, we're in the perfect position to act as conciliators. When we quit thinking of ourselves as adversaries and begin looking out for each other, no one will have to be hurt. And everyone wins—at least a little bit." Rob grinned at the skeptical look on Angela's face and added, "Anyway, that isn't the half of what Simmons is doing to me! But that doesn't mean I'm not willing to help Kevin. I said I would, and I will."

Angela's dark eyes grew round in amazement, then slowly narrowed to suspicious slits. "I think that you'd better explain yourself, Rob. What else has Simmons got up his sleeve?"

"Paper. Pounds and pounds of paper." Rob winced as he answered.

"Paper? What do you mean by that?" Angela slapped the palms of her hands to the tabletop and glared directly into Rob's eyes. The inquisition wouldn't stop until she had squeezed the entire story from him.

"Actually, the paper belongs to your firm. I didn't realize how much money Henshaw, Radison and Grimes invested in paper—and secretaries to type on it!"

"Rob! Make sense!"

"It's hard to make much sense on three hours' sleep, Angela, but what seems to have occurred is an order by Milton Simmons to your firm to keep me busy—very busy. I'm being snowed under by paperwork. It appears that Simmons has left explicit instructions with someone in your firm to keep me so occupied answering interrogatories and responding to multiple motions that require legal briefs and research that I can't deal with my other clients or work on Hannah Green's defense."

Rob hung his head. Running fingers through the sandy hair, he admitted, "I'm exhausted, Angela. I have to give your firm credit. They do their work. I'm getting behind, just as Simmons planned. I've been telling my other clients that I can't help them until this thing with Hannah is settled, but Angie," Rob turned to her with a plea in his eyes, "they need so much help!"

Frustration emanated from every muscle as Rob began to pace in the confines of the conference room. The strong shoulders Angela so admired seemed stooped, heavy with the burdens of others and his own weariness.

Pained to see Rob weakening, she was still befuddled as to why he would help Kevin under such bizarre circumstances. Angela reached beyond herself and did something that amazed even her. As if listening to a stranger on a tape recording, she heard her voice saying: "Well, then *I'll* take on some of your clients! Send them to me!"

"What?" Rob spun to face her, disbelief written across his features. "You're kidding, aren't you? You shouldn't joke about this, Angela. It's very serious."

She spoke again, amazing herself as much as Rob, "I'm not joking. If you have any clients who can get to my office, I'll take them on. You can have them back, of course, when all of this is settled." Angela's lips quivered with a bit of a smile. At least this strange new voice of hers had a sense of humor. Then the old, familiar Angela added, "I don't know why I said that, Rob, but I mean it. I'll help you out. If you can put yourself on the line for Kevin, it's the least I can do."

Rob grinned, some of the old spark back in his eyes. "Deal! I knew you had it in you, Angie! You're not that icy society lawyer down to the core, after all! I knew there was some humanity in there somewhere!"

With that, Angela took a flying swing at her playful tormentor. Missing widely, she lost her balance and stumbled into his broad arms just as Jerry Wilson entered the room.

Mortified by her position, Angela struggled to free herself, but with every movement, Rob tightened his grasp. Then he began to explain the circumstances to the highly amused parole officer. "Miss Malone just insisted on showing her gratitude for my helpful suggestions. But I know you have work for us now, Jerry. So if she'll promise to continue this later, I'll let her go."

Angela squirmed in the cozy grip, acutely embarrassed, but somehow reluctant to have Rob relinquish his grasp. "Let me go!" she hissed, more out of obligation to Jerry Wilson than to her own emotions.

"And *can* we finish this later?" Rob's voice pummeled softly on her eardrum.

"No! Yes! I don't know!" Angela wailed.

"I heard a yes in there, and that's good enough for me. Just don't forget that oral contracts are binding." The silken grip loosened, and Angela found her footing. Physical balance came far more quickly than emotional equilibrium, but for Jerry Wilson's sake, she smoothed the cascading pageboy and squared her shoulders.

"You'll have to excuse Mr. Jordan. His sense of humor seems to be mutating rapidly as we speak." She shot Rob a withering look, which he received with equanimity.

"That's part of his charm, Miss Malone. But then, perhaps I don't have to tell you of Rob's charms?" Wilson parried, enjoying the polished lady laywer's discomfiture. Then, turning back to the business at hand, the parole officer announced, "I have the arresting officer here. Perhaps we should speak to him about Kevin."

The door swung open, and a burly, red-haired lawman in blue sauntered through.

"Officer Cassidy, I'd like you to meet Kevin Simmons' attorney, Miss Angela Malone." Angela found her hand being enveloped by a warm and meaty fist. "And you've met Rob Jordan before."

Nodding in recognition, the officer cast a glance toward Rob before turning his lionlike head back to Angela. She felt herself being appraised by pale eyes and scored on an illusive mental checklist.

Nervously, Angela loosed herself from his grasp. Here was the man who held Kevin's immediate fate. She felt Rob angling toward her. His arm shot out from around her and gripped the now dangling hand of the officer.

"Hi, Bill, how's it going?"

"Okay, Mr. Jordan. And you?"

"Been better, been worse. What's the scoop on the Simmons kid?"

"Let's sit down and discuss it," Jerry Wilson broke in. "We have some things to settle."

Once seated around the battered table, Angela sat back and watched as Rob bargained for their future.

"As the arresting officer are you planning to make formal charges, Cassidy?" Rob turned to face the big man.

"I've been discussing the situation with Wilson, here. The boy isn't charged yet, and I won't bring formal charges if he, as Kevin's probation officer, approves."

All eyes turned toward the slender man. "We've

gone over that already. We'll release Kevin if you'll agree to work with him, Rob. You've had successes with less promising juveniles than Kevin. Officer Cassidy and I are willing to keep this informal as long as we can. So it's up to you."

Rob leaned back in the battered chair and closed his eyes for a moment before answering. "Then it's the only thing to do, wouldn't you say?"

"Good!" Wilson exclaimed, "it's settled then. We'll release Kevin to Miss Malone on these conditions. Rob, you'll oversee his probation with me and get him into whatever program you see fit. Of course you understand, Miss Malone," and Angela found all eyes on her, "that the boy will be released on the condition that he, too, will cooperate. When he ceases to cooperate with you and Mr. Jordan for any reason you are to report to me, as his probation officer, immediately. At that time I will be forced to file a recommendation for the revocation of his probation."

So it all depended on Kevin—and Rob. Angela glanced at him from the corner of her eye. His head was bowed, eyes closed. *Praying again!* Angela rolled her eyes in horror. He picked the most inconvenient times for such nonsense! But Cassidy and Wilson seemed unperturbed by the event. It was apparent they had known Rob for a long time.

*Maybe I'll get used to this, too, but I doubt it.* Angela busied herself with her briefcase, and when she looked up, Rob was gazing at her, amusement apparent in his firmament-colored eyes.

He could read her thoughts, she decided, but he would never change this part of his life for her. Either she would have to grow to understand it or she and Rob could never have any more of a relationship than existed between them now. That thought sent a surprising chill through her. She had spent three weeks away from the aggravating man and found she hated it. She would have to consider carefully what

91

made Rob Jordan tick before she made more fun of it. He really did live this religion stuff.

Rob unfolded himself from the chair and thanked the two officers for their help. As they left the room, he turned to Angela.

"Well, ready to go and get our proverbial 'bad boy?' They'll have him out front in about five minutes."

"In a minute. I think we have something to discuss first."

"We'll have the topic of Kevin Simmons worn out pretty soon, Angela. Maybe we should include him in the next discussion."

"This doesn't concern Kevin. It's you I want to talk about." Angela tapped the tip of her pen against the tabletop in a nervous staccato beat. She felt a bit traitorous in what she was about to say.

"Then talk away, Miss Malone."

"I think you should get a protective order from the court to limit the scope of discovery on this Simmons case. You have the right to request that forthcoming depositions are at a reasonable time and place and at reasonably spaced intervals. Otherwise you might be facing day-long depositions every day for the next two months. Milton Simmons wants to harass you, and he's found a very effective tool unless you put a stop to it."

"Is that the advice I'm hearing from an employee of Henshaw, Radison and Grimes?" Rob's eyebrow quirked in obvious surprise.

"Just don't tell them I said so. You look terrible, Rob. Lack of sleep doesn't become you. For reasons that I cannot understand, you are helping the son of a known adversary, a totally hostile party. You have to give yourself time for that. Get that protective order!"

"Maybe you're right. It's been rough these last few days. And it's Kevin who will benefit in the long run." Rob's shoulders slumped in weariness.

"Good! At least you can get enough rest to stay healthy. Sometimes I can't imagine what makes you tick," Angela observed, bafflement apparent in her tone.

"Can't you, Angela? Not yet?" His tone was so soft that she barely heard the question.

Steeling herself against the inevitable sermon, she answered, "No, Rob. I really don't. I don't understand this religion stuff at all. Though I'm eternally grateful that you're helping Kevin and me, I still don't see why you're doing it. I'd want to be as far away from every part of the Simmons family as I could get!"

"Have you ever read the book of Matthew, Angela?" Rob leaned across the table toward her.

"No, . . . not really." Angela's mind flew to her Sunday morning trek through her grandmother's Bible.

"It explains a lot of things about me, Angela. In one chapter a lawyer asks Jesus this question, 'Which is the great commandment in the law?' Do you know what Jesus told him?"

Angela shook her head slowly, spellbound by the intense look in Rob's eyes.

"He said, 'You shall love the Lord your God with all your heart, and with all your soul, and with all your mind. This is the first, great commandment. And a second is like it, You shall love your neighbor as yourself.' You can't get any more explicit than that, Angela."

"And you believe that means people like Milt Simmons?" Angela queried, doubt suffusing her features.

"I do. And I have to act on it."

Angela sat quietly across from him, admiring the strongly etched cheekbones and the persistently tousled wheat-hued hair. He was as ruggedly handsome and tenderly gentle as any man she had ever met. And

93

the greatest enigma. What powered Rob Jordan, gave him more strength of character and resilience in the face of adversity than she could imagine? Even she, Angela Malone, had to wonder about this God who meant so much to him.

Shattering the somber moment, Rob smiled brightly, a glimpse of sunlight slipping from behind the clouds, illuminating the room and Angela's heart. "Let's go get our boy, Angie. I have a feeling he's had enough of this place."

Kevin met them in front of the precinct desk, looking young and wary, like a small untamed animal unwillingly cornered, awaiting his captors. Jerry Wilson hovered nearby.

"I have explained to Kevin the circumstances of his release. He's agreed to the rules I set forth. He'll be answering to both of you. Feel free to call me if for some reason," and the parole officer gave Kevin a look fraught with meaning, "he doesn't care to continue doing that. Other arrangements will then have to be made."

The euphemisms were not lost on the boy who cowered nearer to Angela. His braggadocio evaporated, but a suspicious look lingered in the clouded eyes.

"Ready?" Rob approached the boy cautiously, cognizant of the apprehensive feelings he might have.

"Do I have a choice?" Kevin challenged, hanging on to the shred of pride he had left.

"Do you want one?" Rob countered. "I thought Mr. Wilson had explained the choices."

Kevin's shoulders slumped dejectedly. All the balls were in Rob's court. He wouldn't even be in the game if it weren't for Mr. Jordan.

"Come on. Angela and I were just going for something to eat—an early supper. Hungry?" Rob caught Angela's eye over Kevin's head. Apparently this was their chance to face him together. After returning Angela's car to her apartment, they found a nearby pancake house.

It was a quiet meal.

Kevin's defiance grew as the meal progressed, challenging any and everything either she or Rob said. While Rob's patience seemed unending, Angela found herself biting the inside of her cheek, willing self-control to prevent her from giving the boy a much needed tongue-lashing. It was with relief that they left him in the hands of the Simmonses' maid with instructions that he was not to go out until the school bus stopped at the end of the block the next morning.

"Do you think I should come and take him to school, Rob?" Angela worried. "Do you think the trouble will start again tomorrow?"

"We have to trust him a little bit. If he skips school tomorrow after an afternoon in jail, he's more foolish than I thought. If his behavior is ever going to be exemplary, it should be now."

Angela sighed and leaned back against the headrest. She smiled secretly as she felt her head touch the sturdy forearm that had slipped behind her. It was wonderful to be with Rob again. She had been a fool to send him away.

"A penny for your thoughts."

"It's no wonder you're so broke, spending money so unwisely!"

He grinned in the oncoming darkness. "Maybe I won't have to pay. Maybe I can guess. I'd like to think that they're similar to my thoughts." A hand curled into the silky hair at the base of her neck.

Angela exhaled in a blissful little gust when she felt Rob's lips nuzzling at her nape, teasing her earlobes with gentle nibbles. Cold-hot shivers bolted through her body like tiny jags of lightning, awakening hidden emotions.

"Do I have to pay up, or did I guess those thoughts for myself?" Rob inquired in her ear.

Hardly able to contain the shudders that his touch sent through her, Angela moaned in soft acquiescence.

"I thought so." Rob took the utterance for his answer and turned her head toward his own, capturing the willing lips before him.

She wanted him as much as he wanted her. It was apparent. But Rob, struggling with his need and the respect he had for her was torn between embracing her fully and pulling back, biding his time. She was far too precious to be treated capriciously. Finally his esteem for her became victor in the war raging within him.

Just as Angela fully relaxed, enjoying the tantalizing exploration of Rob's mouth, he pulled away with a frustrated sigh.

Bemused, her lips still hungering for the taste of his, she turned to him, "Rob, what's wrong? What did I do?"

"You? Nothing! And that's what I'd like to do as well. I'd like nothing better than to spend the rest of the evening parked here in my trusty Volkswagen, with you in my arms. But I can't. Even if a protective order is granted, I have enough work to keep me busy for days. Estine is having problems getting money for child support; twenty-five others are depending on me to solve their problems; and Hannah Green's case is crying for attention. I've got to get some of it done between now and school dismissal tomorrow afternoon. Kevin is going to get so much attention he'll think he's the president, but I've got to find time to do it."

Rob's arm slipped away from Angela's shoulders and she felt suddenly chilly, like a warm winter wrap had been stolen from her. As much as she hated to admit it, Rob was right. This was no time for them to indulge themselves. And if she were going to take on Rob's extra clients as she had offered, her own time demands were going to mount. Milton Simmons had managed to infiltrate every aspect of their lives. And they had to see that no more damage than necessary was done.

"When will I see you?" Angela surprised herself with the question. She was still not accustomed to the longing that Rob fostered in her.

"Friday. For supper. Pick up Kevin at his house, and we'll go to Casa Bonita."

Dinner with Kevin—tacos. Well, it was better than TV dinners on a tray. She slid toward the passenger door and then remembered the little Volkswagen's idiosyncrasies. "Want to let me out?" she asked.

"Not very badly, but I'd better." Rob jumped out and ran around to her side of the car and tugged. A metallic shriek rent the air, and the door fell open. Returning to the driver's seat, Rob waved as the car gasped and jerked to life.

Sadly she watched the bug disappear into city traffic.

The days passed slowly. Irate phone calls from school officials did nothing to appease her nervousness. She thought back to a conversation of this morning.

"Miss Malone? This is Alvin Worthington. I'm superintendent of the school at which Kevin Simmons is registered."

Angela's heart had plummeted at the salutation.

"Yes, Mr. Worthington, what can I do for you?"

"Your name was given to me by the maid at Kevin's home. Apparently his parents are on an extended business trip, and the boy was left in the housekeeper's charge. We've been having some difficulties with him and wanted to set up a conference. She said that you were the one I should call."

*Yes, every boy needs legal help for a school conference. Every boy whose father is Milt Simmons.*

Fury mounted within Angela. So she and the Simmonses' maid had been left in charge—without Angela's knowledge.

"Another friend of Kevin's and I are planning to take him out for supper tonight, Mr. Worthington. If you can give me some idea of the problems, perhaps we could deal with them tonight."

"He's come very close to suspension, Miss Malone. It's primarily an attitude problem. He's been skipping classes and fighting with his teachers. His grades have taken a nosedive. He's a bright boy, Miss Malone. I hate to see this happening. If there's any way we can work together to salvage this young man, I'd like to do it."

"Thank you, Mr. Worthington. Those are my thoughts exactly. Either I or a Mr. Robert Jordan will be contacting you about Kevin. I'd like to have the opportunity to discuss the situation with both of them before we take any action."

"Jordan? Robert Jordan, did you say? Well! That puts a whole new light on things!" Mr. Worthington's tone held new relief.

"What?" Angela suddenly felt she had lost the thread of the conversation.

"I've worked with Mr. Jordan before, Miss Malone. He's very active in a rehabilitation program for teens and has done some volunteer coaching of Little League baseball and worked with the Boy Scouts. In fact, we go to the same church. The children like him very much. If he's going to be involved with Kevin, that sets my mind at ease."

*Rob strikes again.* No wonder he didn't have time for himself, time to rest. He gave it all away—and never even mentioned it. He really did live what he believed, quietly and humbly. He had become more of a mystery than ever. What motivated him so? Surely not that Christianity he espoused! Ridiculous!

Angela spent the remainder of her morning pensively musing. She was anxious to hear what Rob and Kevin had to say to each other tonight. She idly fingered the one-carat amethyst gemstone dangling from a gold chain around her neck. She had purchased it as an investment, but admired it more as a pretty bauble. Its color and its exotic origin had attracted her. But now she had even forgotten that—Bangkok? Zambia? Rio? Sri Lanka? Just one more possession to be cared for and stored. She could have purchased a dozen of pairs of shoes for Rob with the check she had written for this one tiny gem. Were her priorities so vastly different that it would tear them apart? Time would tell.

Kevin was sullen and quiet in Angela's car as they sped toward Casa Bonita. Angela was relieved to see Rob waiting under the stucco arches of the restaurant as she pulled in.

"Well, there's Rob. And here's a parking spot, right in front. What luck!"

"Big deal." Kevin looked disgusted with the entire situation. Angela knew she had dragged him from the cavern of his room and the dark, pulsating beat of some unpleasant rock group. The maid had looked harried and concerned. She had admitted in whispered tones that Kevin only left his room when forced. To Angela that was a foreboding sign.

"Hi, Kev, how's it going?" Rob greeted Kevin and waved a salute toward Angela. "Are you hungry? Tacos, burritos? What do you have in mind?" Rob grabbed the reluctant boy by the shoulders and steered him into the restaurant, forcing compliance.

Later, as Rob pushed the last of the plates away and leaned back in his chair, he commented, "I talked to Mr. Worthington today."

Kevin shot a malevolent look Rob's way. "So what did the old goat want?"

"What did *who* want?" Irritation crackled in Rob's voice.

"The old . . . Mr. Worthington."

"He says that you're having trouble at school."

"If those teachers would quit hassling me, everything would be fine."

"He says you've been skipping classes."

"Hey, man! It's boring! What a drag. Those teachers don't know nothing!"

"Don't know nothing, huh?" Rob prodded. "Is that what I'm hearing from the fellow that pulled straight A's in English last year?"

"They don't know *anything*—well, they don't!"

"So you've been fighting with them, right?"

"They're blaming me for things I don't do. I gotta stand up for myself!"

Angela watched the inquisition with grudging admiration. Rob knew how to handle Kevin. The boy hadn't won a point at any turn so far.

"And the craziest thing that Worthington told me was that you're failing in most of your classes!"

"What's so crazy about that? They've got it in for me! Those teachers all hate me. I can tell."

"Don't give me that, Kevin. We both know better than that." Rob allowed anger to tinge his voice for the first time.

The boy cowered slightly before trying one final ploy. "So maybe I have a learning disability! Maybe I can't do it! Didya ever think of that?"

Rob gave a whoop of humorless laughter. "Kevin Simmons, if you have a learning disability, I have a billion dollars in my checking account! I've looked at your records. Your IQ is one of the highest in the school. Academically your performance has been flawless until last year. Sorry, Kevin, you can't *catch* a learning disability. Want to try any more shoddy excuses?"

Angela watched as Rob shouldered his way closer to Kevin, admiring the vast, muscular expanse of his back. Vexation played across his exquisite features.

100

He would be frightening except that both she and Kevin knew that Rob was a very tender man.

But Rob was not allowing this trait to stand in the way of what Kevin needed to hear. Controlled fury sparked his words.

"Listen to me! You're paving a path to self-destruction, Kevin. And I want you to stop. It's time you started taking responsibility for your own actions and their consequences. Do you know what that means?"

Kevin shook his head sullenly.

"Well, then I'll tell you. You'd better sign up for a tutor and get your classwork back on track. And that means being in school every day—all day long. If you don't hold up your end of the bargain, I won't feel obligated to hold up mine. And your parole officer has told you the results of that."

A defiant, pouty look had been growing on the boy's face as Rob spoke. Suddenly Kevin pushed himself away from the table and stood.

"So let me go to jail! You don't care, not really! Neither does *she!*" and he pointed an accusing finger at Angela. "And we all know that my folks don't. So take the easy way out. Let me rot somewhere. Nobody will ever miss me!" Then he turned and ran, dodging tables and waiters as he went.

Rob threw his wallet across the table at Angela. "Take care of this. I'll collect later. I'll get it back tomorrow. I have to go after him." With that, Rob darted after the boy, his athletic profile disappearing into a cluster of patrons at the front of the café.

"It's hopeless!" Angela stormed aloud as she counted bills from Rob's worn wallet. She would tell Rob so tomorrow. It wouldn't be difficult to find another job when Simmons had her fired. She was a fine attorney. And it would be much easier than living on the emotional roller-coaster ride that Kevin kept her on.

Counting mindlessly, Angela pulled bills and scraps

of paper from the wallet until she had enough for Rob's portion of the bill. She would pay for herself and Kevin—an appropriate farewell meal. She was darkly amused that Rob's wallet was full of dollar bills—so unlike the men she knew whose smallest change was always a fifty. On top of the pitiful paper stack was a shred of notepaper inscribed with Rob's familiar scrawl—KIM—and a local telephone number. Barely curious as to who this Kim might be, she stuffed the scrap into the wallet before she closed it. Then throwing money down for her own meal and the tip, she stood to leave.

She'd tell Rob to give up tomorrow when she returned the billfold. Their plan to help Kevin would never work—and she had to convince Rob of that. It was hopeless.

## CHAPTER 7

STILL IN A BLUE FUNK about the prior evening, Angela set out for Rob's office to return the wallet. She found herself fingering the worn folder, relishing the soft, scarred leather. She would have tossed it into the garbage had she found it on the street. It was old and tattered, but because it was Rob's, she found it priceless.

Driving through the city streets, she rehearsed what she would say to dissuade him from continuing with Kevin's rehabilitation.

"It's no good, Rob. He's incorrigible. . . ."

No, Rob would never accept the theory.

"We can't do it alone. Without help from his home, our efforts will be useless. . . ."

Rob wouldn't agree.

She couldn't see a way to convince him, but she knew deep in her heart that it was no use. Kevin was beyond saving.

It was on that glum note that Angela pulled up in front of Rob's tattered office building only to see Kevin in jeans and a Chicago Bears sweatshirt, backing out of the front door carrying an office desk. Soon Rob appeared, balancing the other end and giving directions as Kevin backed down the littered staircase.

"Hi, Angela! You're just in time! The big stuff is out and we need every hand we can get to carry boxes. Why don't you take the plants for us? Kevin says they make him sneeze."

Angela stood, feet planted like saplings, staring at the untroubled scene. Had she traveled through a time-warp or was this actually less than twenty-four hours since the turbulent scene at Casa Bonita?

"Close your mouth and join the fun." Rob whispered in Angela's ear as he guided the desk, closing her gaping mouth with a warm, dusty finger. He was in wash-worn, snug-fitting jeans that rode low on his hips. His short-sleeved white knit shirt was pulling out of his pants in back and a streak of dirt meandered from under his left arm and down over the muscular curve of his hip. He was powdered with a fine dust, courtesy of the storm they stirred up as they moved furniture down the seldom vacuumed halls.

Tousled and dusty, free of pretension, and so blatantly masculine it nearly took her breath away, Rob Jordan was blissfully unaware of the sensual response he awakened in Angela. But even more astounding than that was the cheerful face of Kevin Simmons grinning at her through an equally liberal smattering of dust.

"All right, you guys. What's going on here?" Angela put her hands on her hips and squared off against the two of them.

"We're moving. I found another office for one-eighth the current rent here. It's only a few blocks away, too. So everything should work out great."

"I mean, about you two. Last night you were at each other's throats. Today you're a team. What happened?"

"Kevin and I had a little discussion. He made a few decisions about his life—in and out of jail, that is. I guess *not* being with me is even worse than being with me!" Rob commented wryly.

Mentally Angela nodded, having discovered the same statement could apply to her own feelings, but aloud she responded, "Well, I don't have clue one what happened between last night and this morning, but I won't argue! I'm no fool! I won't tamper with success!"

"Good girl. Come and tamper with some of these boxes instead. I've got plans for this afternoon and I want to finish moving by noon."

The three of them hauled and carried until nothing was left in the sunshine yellow office but a lone fly buzzing pitifully against a windowpane. With obvious relish, Rob pulled the door shut on his old office and his ex-landlord, Milton Simmons.

"Now, then. On to the new place. Angela, would you like to come? Or do you want to rest for this afternoon?"

Angela's forehead furrowed. "This afternoon? What's so special about this afternoon?"

Rob chuckled before his spoke. "I did that backward, didn't I? I'm sorry. I meant to ask you last night and forgot in all the confusion with Kevin. The local bar association is sponsoring a golf tournament this afternoon. Tee off is every five minutes. Entry fee includes a steak fry. Want to go? That is, I mean, you *do* play golf, don't you?"

Angela was suddenly and overwhelmingly grateful for an older brother who had recruited his younger sister as caddie at the age of eight. By the time Angela was fifteen, she was giving her brother Peter a run for his money on the links. Now Peter rarely called her to golf. Too humiliating, he said, to be beaten by his baby sister.

"I do and I will! I haven't had my clubs out for

several weeks, but I'm sure I'll figure out how to use them within a hole or two!"

Rob smiled, his even white teeth flashing. "I haven't golfed all summer. Too much to do. But everyone deserves a day off now and then. You convinced me of it last night. Anyway, this is a charity tournament—a favorite of mine. I'd like to be there."

"But what about Kevin? Do you dare leave him?"

"You mean, will he pull a Dr. Jekyll and Mr. Hyde routine and turn into monster child again? I doubt it. Anyway, he has a date for the afternoon—with a tutor. He's got enough algebra and chemistry to keep him busy. He's a good kid. He just needs to know the limits. I think I laid them out pretty clearly for him. Plus, I promised him Sunday. We're going to spend it together."

Angela felt a twinge of envy. Lucky Kevin. A whole day with Rob. Then, mentally chastising herself, she recalled that today was *her* day with Rob. She'd better not waste a minute of it.

"When does the tournament begin?"

"Two o'clock. Can you pick me up? The trunk of the Volkswagen won't hold two sets of clubs with carts. I can be sitting on my front steps by one-thirty."

"Sure, but I think I'll go home and get ready now. I don't want to strain my swing lifting any more boxes."

Rob nodded in cheerful agreement and trotted off on rubber-soled feet, waving back over his head as he departed.

Grinning, Angela climbed into her car and pulled away. *What a man. A real novelty.* No masculine insecurities there. He was the first man who had ever asked her to pick *him* up. And she loved it. Rob Jordan didn't need money or power to give him the illusion of authority. He was the complete male.

Promptly at one-thirty, Angela pulled up in front of

Rob's apartment building. As promised, he was perched on the front step, freshly showered and wearing khaki pants and a khaki and powder-blue striped shirt.

The blue in the shirt brought out the blue in his eyes, like sparkling stars against his lightly tanned face. He looked so wholesome, yet blatantly sensual, lounging there, that, had another woman come along just then, Angela knew her head would turn for another look as she passed by.

*Wholesome!* Angela suddenly realized what she was thinking. This was a quality she had never looked for in a man. Wealth, yes. Power, always. Wholesomeness, never. What was Rob Jordan doing to her? He was jarring her values, making her question her priorities, rocking the foundation of her purpose in life. No wonder he could influence Kevin so dramatically.

*Forewarned is forearmed*, Angela thought to herself. She had never let Rob alter her beliefs or actions. She would have to think of him as an adversary, albeit a tender one, if she were to preserve her own convictions. The effect of his churchy leanings could be controlled as long as she was constantly on guard.

Throwing introspection to the wind then, she waved at Rob, who jumped from his perch, swung a set of golf clubs over his shoulder, and trotted toward the car.

"Hi! Ready to play?" Rob tossed the clubs into the back seat with a clatter that made Angela wince.

"Can you play at all with those old things?" She eyed the antiquated sticks in the back seat.

"Sure. My dad used them for twenty years, and he's a terrific golfer. The way I see it, he trained them for me. I should have a twenty-year practice advantage over everyone else."

"Well, if it works for you. . . ."

"It does. I don't mind old clubs. You should know

that by now." Rob squirmed into a comfortable position against the leather headrest.

"It seems the more I learn about you, the less I know. Figure that out."

"I'm a simple man, Angela. Don't make me into someone complex. Even my religion is simple. It's based on faith, simple faith. God offers—I accept. Nothing more complicated than that."

Much to Angela's relief, the Saturday afternoon traffic diminished as they neared the club, and Rob's mind turned to the upcoming match. They would have to avoid talking religion if she were to enjoy the afternoon.

The clubhouse spread before them like a Tudor mansion, full of turrets and decorative battens. The pale tan stucco gleamed from beneath curling ivy and vines winding their way up the walls like a deep green blanket. Emerald fairways stretched as far as the eye could see across rolling hills and through lush tree stands.

"This is a lovely course! I've never golfed here. My brother and I usually played at one across town," Angela exclaimed.

"Dad and I have played here ever since I was nine. He's a member, but I've never been able to afford it."

Questions niggled at the back of Angela's mind. "Rob, you rarely mention your family. All I know is that your mother is an interior decorator and your father is a member of this golf club."

"That's more than I know about you. You'll meet my family someday. My mother is the flamboyant one. Dad's the serious thinker. That's why he plays golf. To escape. Otherwise Mom would have him moving furniture and hanging pictures all day long."

Angela couldn't imagine Rob in that family portrait, but she shrugged and said, "My family is very much like me—upwardly mobile. Dad's a businessman; Mom's what she likes to call a 'socialite'; and my brother Peter is a commodity broker."

"So who taught you to play golf—your Dad or Peter?"

Angela grinned wickedly as she answered, "Peter. And be thankful I'm your partner. He says I'm good."

Rob beamed at her. "Then what are we waiting for? I think I hear a hole-in-one calling us!"

Laughing, they set off for the tee box, Rob's battered clubs clanking along next to Angela's gleaming graphite ones.

Angela was unaccountably self-conscious as she teed off on hole one. Perhaps it was the affectionate observer lounging on a redwood bench waiting his turn. She had never before felt so self-conscious of the curve of her legs in shorts or the gracefulness of her posture as she played. Relief flooded through her as she heard the club head and ball connect with a resounding thwack that meant good distance for her first shot. Finally daring to look up from the point at which her ball had rested, she saw the little white bullet sailing straight down the fairway, dead center. It landed some two hundred yards from where she stood, clean and trouble-free.

"Very impressive!" came a voice from behind her. Rob's was the only one she heard, then slowly it dawned on her that the golfers behind her were clapping.

She exhaled deeply, rolling her eyes in relief. Rob stepped up to the tee box, a one wood in hand and took a practice swing. The muscles rippled through his shoulders and neck as he swung, trim hips turning the direction of the flag in perfect form. Teeing the ball high, Rob then addressed it, settling his club behind it in studious concentration. Slowly, with animal grace, he lifted the club behind him until it hung poised over his right shoulder and neck. The club glinted in the sunlight as it arced in powerful trajectory. A resonant crack proclaimed a square hit, and a sibilant sound could be heard among the several spectators.

Rob's ball bounced within ten feet of the green and settled at the top of a grassy knoll, waiting to be chipped in.

"Did you see that?"

"What a drive!"

"I can see who's going to give last year's winners a run for their money!"

"Now there's a team!"

Rob's eyes twinkled as he turned to his partner. "Lucky shot. I usually whiff."

The hoots and catcalls behind him reminded him that others were listening.

"You'd better start whiffing mighty quick, Jordan. Otherwise, you might win this match. Then you'd have to take a trophy home. We'd hate to see that happen!"

Rob took the ribbing good-naturedly as he stuffed his club into the worn bag. Then putting his hand on Angela's elbow he said, "Come on partner. We'd better go chase down those balls."

The piquant smell of freshly mowed grass teased Angela's nostrils as they sauntered down the fairway. A light breeze ruffled her hair and brought with it the heady smell of a patch of flowers growing in a riot of color behind a nearby tee box.

"It's wonderful out here, Rob! I'm so glad you asked me to come!" Angela said enthusiastically.

"It is spectacular, isn't it? That's why I keep golfing, even though it takes more time and money than I have to spare. It gets me out into Nature and makes me marvel at God's handiwork."

Angela cast a warning glance Rob's way, but he was already onto another tack, lining up her ball with the flag at the green.

"You're going to have to play this one uphill. That's always deceiving. The hole is farther away than it looks. I'd use a seven iron."

"Right, boss." Angela agreed, relieved that Rob was distracted from his sermonette. She punched the ball up the hill and it landed on the apron, near Rob's ball.

As he lined up his next shot, Angela couldn't help but admire his trim hips and sturdy legs, moving effortlessly until he had secured his stance. His physique was as flawless as his golf game and he chipped the ball into the hole.

"An eagle! Rob, that's wonderful!"

At the fourth hole, Rob and Angela's score card was a series of impressive pars and birdies, but their concentration was sorely tested as they came upon two backed-up teams and were forced to wait to tee off.

They found a bench nestled under an arch of oak trees, half-hidden from the traffic on the course. Rob threw himself down on the bench and patted the seat beside him.

"Come on. We've got a bit of a wait here."

Angela settled next to him, glad to scurry into the warmth of his waiting embrace. Soon she felt him nuzzle her silky locks and she tipped her head to meet his lips.

They were startled apart by the golfers behind them, watching with some amusement the brief tryst.

"No wonder you two golf so well together. You do everything well together." The dry comment forced them apart as effectively as a battering ram.

"Are we supposed to be teeing off?" Rob asked, grinning stupidly and running his fingers through his hair.

"Yup. We hated to interrupt you, but this hole seems to be a bottleneck. There's a wooden rain shelter on hole seven. If you golf fast enough, you can have five minutes there before we catch up with you."

Rob laughed aloud at the playful ribbing and pulled a mortified Angela from the bench.

Thoughts of those last few minutes seemed to infuse their play after that with a lazy, carefree attitude. The competitiveness was gone and Rob, playing with less intensity, spent more time smiling at his partner and less lining up his shots. Angela, more competitive, struggled to regain the hunger to win, but each time she remembered Rob's lips on hers, her mind wandered away from the game and to the sensations that ebbed and flowed through her at Rob's touch.

Tallying their scores at the day's end, Angela whispered into Rob's ear. "We have a good chance of winning, Rob! If you hadn't gotten that bogie on hole seven, our scores would be terrific!"

"I couldn't concentrate on that hole, Angela, I couldn't quit thinking about you at that rain shelter."

Angela's face mottled to a deep red as she remembered their minutes there together. It had been a wonderful interlude, but it had certainly thrown Rob's game off. . . .

Angela's hand tightened around Rob's wrist as the local bar president stepped up to announce the winners. Her grip slackened as she heard their names announced in second place. Disappointment welled through her. They had played well enough to capture first! If only Rob had taken the game more seriously!

She found herself being propelled through the crowd until she was standing in front of the trophy winners raising their booty and accepting gracious kudos from those around them.

Rob stepped in front of them and stuck out a hand in congratulations. "Good job, guys! Now we know who the best golfers are. Next year I'll know who to watch out for!" Rob was obviously delighted for the pair.

"So will we, Jordan. If you and Ms. Malone get any better, we're going to have to take some lessons!"

Immersed in playful banter, Rob could not see the storm clouds brewing on Angela's face.

Finally turning away from the congratulatory scene, he came face to face with Angela, dark eyes shooting angry daggers his way.

"What's wrong, Angela? What happened?" Rob asked, concern heavy in his voice.

"Don't you know?" Inflectionless, Angela's voice took on an edge of steel.

"No. But I'd better find out." Pulling her from the crowd, Rob worked their way to a secluded corner. Edging Angela into it, he faced her squarely. "So, what's going on? You look like you could kill."

"Rob Jordan, you idiot! What was all that nonsense about 'now we know who the better golfers are?' *We're* the better golfers! They should never have had that trophy. If we'd been tending to business instead of fooling around in that rain shelter, that trophy would have been ours!"

"So what, Angela? We had fun, didn't we? And they shot a better score. Big deal."

"And you seem perfectly happy about it!"

"I am. We came in second. I think that's terrific, especially as little as I've golfed recently." Rob shrugged lightly.

"How can you take this so casually? Don't you understand? *We could have won!*"

"No one else seems to care who won or lost—only you," Rob reminded her.

Angela tugged at a strand of hair in frustration. "Don't you see, Rob. When you're climbing a corporate ladder, you don't have time for just fun! People are watching—everything you do counts. We should have made more of an effort to win. It's image. Success! That's the name of the game!"

Rob stared at the irate girl in amazement, then he answered softly, "It's not the name of *my* game, Angela." He shook his head slowly from side to side in a physical refutation of Angela's claim.

"Well it should be! How else can people judge your

113

worth but by your work and by the way you present yourself?''

"I wish you'd try to understand." Rob took her silence for approval to continue. "Angela, to me earthly standards don't apply. How people look or dress or spend money doesn't matter to me. You should know that by now. Jesus reminds us that to be first in His Kingdom, we must be willing to be last. What happens in this world—whether we're first or last, powerful or weak, rich or poor, isn't really all that important."

Angela's eyes darted from side to side, looking for eavesdroppers. She wished Rob wouldn't be so *open* about all this. But she couldn't bring herself to silence him. His words were making her think.

"Give God your excellence, Angela. Don't worry about what others may think. And remember, the real purpose is to *serve* others, not to *conquer* them. Christ teaches us to love our neighbors as ourselves and do good for our enemies. I know that lawyers are always generally thought to be out to win! But it's like I said before. I finally decided the best way to practice law was through reconciliation. That way, both sides could win, both sides could leave my office with their heads held high." Rob chucked her under the chin. "Don't look so surprised, Angela. We should be doing it all the time. Our canon of professional ethics teaches us that we have a duty in every divorce case to explore the possibility of reconciliation for each couple. Why not in other situations as well?"

Angela's internal fury abating, she leaned into the wall, staring at the beguiling, handsome face before her. More and more she felt drawn to this dear and selfless man. And less and less could she understand him.

"Hey! You guys want a steak, or are you in the corner, pouting because you didn't win?"

Rob turned toward the source of the good-natured ribbing. "Nah, giving them a scare was enough fun for me. Where's the steak? Is this a do-it-yourself outfit?"

Promptly a platter came their way, loaded with inch-thick T-bones that covered all but the outside rim of the plate.

"There's an open spot on the grill if you move fast, Jordan. If you wait any longer, you'll wind up having to pray for a space!"

Angela's head shot up as Rob laughed and moved toward the grill. So these other attorneys knew about Rob's religious proclivities, too. And they didn't seem to mind! Perhaps it was only she who was so uncomfortable. She'd have to think it over. Possibly it was her own values that needed rethinking.

As if reading her mind, Rob began to speak. "I've surrendered my practice to Him, Angela. Slowly. Painfully. Two steps forward and one step back. I've worried about monthly overhead. I feared that if I turned my practice over to Him, I might go broke. I knew that I was a good money manager, but I wasn't so sure about Him! Finally I left the Smith, Keyes and Lovall firm. At least I wouldn't be a financial detriment to them. My parents cut me off when I did that. They viewed me as a financial disaster. But then, no one ever said it would be easy."

Hesitant to offend, Angela interjected softly, "If this God you love so much loves you, why would He allow you to have such a difficult time, Rob? And why don't you give *yourself* credit for what you've achieved? What I've accomplished professionally I've done by myself. God didn't help me Rob. Maybe he didn't help you either."

Rob smiled sadly. "He's touched my life, Angela. And when it happens, it's a powerful experience. You're never the same again. I'm praying it will happen for you." He ran a gentle finger down her cheek, and his grin widened. He had said his piece and refused to go farther, Angela knew, but the moment had shaken her. She was relieved it was past as Rob began to behave as if there were nothing more pressing on his mind than grilling a steak and securing an empty spot before the fire.

"Ready to leave?" Rob stretched lazily in front of the clubhouse fireplace and rolled toward Angela. She could feel the heat still radiating from his body and the tangy, smoky smell of birch clinging to his clothes. "Shorts are okay for daytime, but it gets pretty chilly at night. It's the lake breeze that does it."

"I'm fine. Your sweater helped. It's so comfortable here, I hate to leave." Angela nestled inside the soft wool sweater Rob had tossed her after dinner. She hesitated to relinquish it, savoring instead the enveloping warmth and the fragrant, earthy aftershave that teased her nostrils when she dipped her head and shoulders deep within the shawl collar.

"I know, but your legs feel like icicles. And remember, you have to drive *me* home tonight. You haven't fulfilled all the responsibilities of your date yet. After all, I have to be walked to my door and kissed goodnight."

Abruptly motivated, Angela uncoiled her legs and sprang to her feet. "Well, then, what are we waiting for? Do you have a curfew? I don't want to be in trouble with your parents!"

Laughingly, Rob followed. "The folks have been pretty lax about curfew these past few years. I think living on the other side of town had something to do with that."

"Oh, good!" Angela mopped her brow in mock relief. "Come on, race you to the car. I can hardly wait to get the heater on!"

"Why don't you wait by the door. I'll bring the car around with the motor warmed. Then those goose-bumps on your legs won't get even more goose-bumps!"

Touched by the thoughtfulness, Angela acquiesced. Unexpected tears pricked at the backs of her eyelids as she dug deep in her pocket for the keys to her car. One trickled down her cheek after Rob had left for the parking lot, and she wiped it away with the back of her hand.

It had been a long time since anyone had been so thoughtful. Angela always demanded that she be treated like an equal—and her wish had been granted. Her pride was in her toughness, her savvy. But gentleness had fallen by the wayside in her quest. And now Rob was providing it. Her gentle opponent. The one she was drawn to but could not understand. Her tender adversary.

The beeping of a horn wrested her from her reverie, and she raced out to the waiting vehicle. Rob leaned over and pushed open the door and she slid inside.

"Brrrrrr! These late summer nights feel more like October!" She shuddered with the cold and attempted to catch the first faint gusts of heat coming through the vents.

"The car will be warm in a minute. How about stopping at my place for a cup of hot chocolate and a pair of jeans to wear home?"

Angela giggled. "Do you think they'd fit?"

"No, but they would make your teeth stop chattering."

"Sold! Can you spare a pair?" Angela knew the meagerness of Rob's wardrobe.

He chuckled deeply. "Now, if you wanted to borrow a *suit*, I might be hesitant, but my closet is *full* of old jeans. You can go in and take your pick."

"It's a deal, but I prefer designer jeans."

Rob picked up on the deprecating humor. "I have clothing from the finest stores in the land. You may be familiar with some of them—J. C. Penney, Sears, K-Mart."

"Okay, okay, that will do. How far are we from your apartment? I haven't been watching." Angela pulled her eyes from the firm jaw and chiseled profile under the mop of sandy hair and glanced at the passing street sign.

"About ten feet from my front door." Rob pulled the car underneath a streetlight only steps from his apartment building.

"My, that was a quick trip!"

"It's the company you're keeping, my dear. Come on, let's get you inside."

"At least it's warm in the hallway," Angela muttered, chilled again by the walk from car to building and regretting the scanty shorts that had felt so good in the afternoon.

"It's warmer in the hall than the apartment most of the winter. It's a good thing I have the genes of a polar bear or I'd have moved out long ago. Hot all summer, cold all winter." With that, Rob flung open the door he had been struggling with and flicked on a light switch around the corner.

Angela stepped into the room, but paused only inches across the threshold, stunned into immobility.

"Rob! What happened?"

The apartment had a whole new look. A tufted couch with decorative pillows sat at one edge of the room. Behind it on a scrolled wooden sofa table gleamed light from a crystal-based lamp. Across the room a matching love seat, flanked by tall wingback chairs. The mauve and navy velvet furniture was accented by lighter violet hue in pillows and accent lamps. Rob moved from behind Angela and toured the room flicking them on as she stared.

Turning to her he shrugged, and explained in a single word, "Mom."

"Your mother did this? It's beautiful!"

"I think she was feeling guilty. She stopped by and saw I didn't have a thing except that broken chair or

118

whatever it was. Don't worry, it's only temporary."
Rob explained as if the appearance and disappearance
of fine furniture were an everyday occurrence.

"Are you sure? This is lovely stuff." Angela traced
an admiring finger across the cording on a couch.

"Positive. She left a note saying not to eat in the
living room. It's a sure sign. I have a theory. When I
get to keep the furniture, she'll let me eat on it. Want
some hot chocolate?"

Angela nodded dumbly and followed him into the
cubbyhole kitchen. She watched him prepare the
cocoa and took a steaming mug to warm her fingers
before she spoke.

"Rob, there's something very strange about your
family."

"Boy! You can say that again!" He spoke in genial
agreement.

"I mean it, Rob! You take for granted that gorgeous
furniture will come and go from your place like it was
a warehouse, yet you hardly have a dime to your
name. I don't get it."

"Right on two counts. This *is* a warehouse for my
mother. She did this all the time I was growing up too.
And I don't get it, either."

"Huh?" Totally baffled, Angela stared at him
across the top of the mug, steam curling upward.

"I don't have a dime to my name most of the time,
and I don't get any from my parents. We tend to
disagree on how to spend money. I like to give mine
away."

"About that—"

"No, Angela, not about that. You can't convince
me to do otherwise, so please don't try." Rob stood
from the chair he had taken and began to pace about
the room.

"I don't want to convince you of anything, Rob. I
just want to understand!"

He must have heard the ring of sincerity in her

119

voice, for just as abruptly as he had stood, he sat down again, across from her and stared into her eyes.

"Remember Matthew?"

"Like in the Bible Matthew?"

"That's the one. There's a wonderful section in chapter five where Jesus is teaching. He compares believers to salt."

"Salt? That sounds a bit ridiculous to me, Rob," Angela scoffed. This religion could really get out of hand.

"It's a perfect analogy because He goes on to ask what good salt is if it's lost its taste."

"Well, it isn't good for anything then!"

"Exactly. It might as well be tossed out and walked on."

"This still doesn't make much sense to me."

"Well, then He compares Christians to light. He calls them the 'light of the world.' "

"This must be catchy. Somehow that sounds more logical than salt." Angela rolled her eyes and Rob grinned. "So tell me more."

"You don't light a lamp and stick it under a basket or in a closet, do you?"

"Of course not! Rob, don't be patronizing!"

"I'm not. I just needed to make a point. When you light a lamp, you put it where it can light the house, where everyone will see it—right?"

"Yes, but what's the point of all of this?"

"Christians are supposed to allow their light to shine, to witness, if you will, to others so they can see their good works and recognize God's hand in them."

"Sounds a bit convoluted to me," Angela commented, her defense weakening. "But what does that mean for you, Rob?"

"I know that you're confused and embarrassed about what I believe and how I live, but it's what I have to do. I feel I've been given wonderful gifts by God, and I'm compelled to serve Him in return. Not because He forces me to, but because I want to. And part of all that is letting the light shine, showing people what it's like to be a Christian."

"But don't you ever tire of that, Rob?" Struggling to understand, Angela leaned forward, cocoa forgotten, deep furrows etching her brow.

Rob laughed delightedly and tweaked her nose. "No! Not at all! Remember, a light by its very nature has to shine—otherwise it isn't a light at all! It isn't hard—it just happens!"

"Well, all I can say is, I wish you wouldn't shine so hard in public. You embarrass me, you know." Angela sat back against the cushions, battling the questions that warred in her mind.

Rob moved across to where she sat and slid down beside her. Pulling her head to his shoulder, he stroked the silky strands of her hair. "You'll understand someday, Angela. I'll give you time. You've come a long way already from the hostile little foe I met in night court."

Angela chuckled softly as she remembered that night that seemed so long ago. Then she felt Rob's lips tracing a pattern from the top of her head, past her temple on an inexorable path to her lips. Her eyes opened wide once with a blissful shudder before Rob closed them with a kiss. And in that fleeting moment she noticed that the bold painted arrow that traversed the room now ended in an oriental vase. Whatever else Rob Jordan might be, he was never dull.

# CHAPTER 8

ANGELA STARTED FROM A DEEP, dreamless slumber. Groggy and disoriented, she sat on the edge of her bed collecting her cobwebby thoughts and wondering what the sound was coming from her front door. Her front door! Someone was tapping a rhythm that was growing louder with each measure.

"Coming! Coming! Hold your fire!" She yelled through the bedroom door, which was standing ajar. Scrambling for a robe, she stumbled toward the offending noise. Pulling on the turquoise gown, she knotted it tightly at her waist and ran widespread fingers through her tangled locks before opening the door.

There stood Rob and Kevin, dressed as though they'd stepped from the pages of *Gentleman's Quarterly*. Kevin's hair was combed and watered down until it lay like a cap around his head. Even Rob had managed to tame his tousled waves, but an errant forelock was inching back to its accustomed spot on his forehead.

"What are you two doing here? It's only nine

o'clock in the morning! Go home and go back to bed." Angela started to push the door shut as Rob's arm shot out to stop her.

"We came to pick you up. Kevin and I thought you might like to spend the day with us."

"My day doesn't start for another three hours yet, thank you. Come and ask me then." Angela yawned and shuffled toward the couch where she curled into a sleepy ball, ignoring her early morning guests.

"Then you'll miss church!"

She opened one eye and gave Rob a baleful glare. "So what else is new?"

He grinned and pulled her unwillingly to her feet. "Go get dressed. We'll wait."

"Oh, no, you don't," she protested warily. "I don't want to go to church, and you can't make me."

"Neither did Kevin, but here he is. You don't want to be a bad example, do you?"

Angela eyed the sulky boy. Maybe Rob was right. If he could convince Kevin, she shouldn't make it any more difficult. "Oh, all right, but don't make a habit of this."

Rob only smiled a lazy, charm-packed smile, making no promises.

Rubbing her eyes with the heel of her hand, Angela stumbled toward her bedroom, shooting an occasional dirty look at Rob who cheerfully ignored them.

Ten minutes later, she stepped once again into the living room, this time in a sleek red tunic of Oriental design. Intricate black braid frogs held the amazing garment together, the last one buttoning at the high mandarin collar. She wore a black platelike hat on the top of her head and her inky hair swung below it like charcoal satin.

Simultaneous whistles cut through the air as the two men on the couch voiced their approval.

"Well, don't just sit there gawking. Let's go and get this over with!" Angela teased, delighted by their response.

123

Rob jumped up with catlike grace and turned to Kevin. "We've got a big responsibility taking this lady out. Think we can live up to it?"

"I guess," Kevin intoned as he struggled to his feet.

"I love enthusiasm in my escorts," Angela commented, poking the boy in the arm as she did so.

"Yeah, we can handle it," he admitted, a smile playing at the corners of his mouth. "If I can dress up in this monkey-suit and go to church, I can do anything."

"Atta, boy! Then let's go." Rob steered the trio out the door and toward his car, parked at the front of the building.

Both Angela's and Kevin's feet were dragging by the time they reached the front portico of Rob's church. The two, each tempted to turn around and run for the car, were stopped only by the cheerful greeting of Jerry Wilson, Kevin's parole officer, who appeared to be an usher for the service. Wilson's obvious delight at seeing the three of them in church together forced them through the massive wooden doors and into the sanctuary.

Rob nudged them toward the front of the building, but Angela, unwilling to go any farther forward, slipped into a pew at the middle. Rob sat between the two of them, marshaling them like a parent with two errant children.

Soon, however, Angela's innate curiosity took over and she began to look around the sanctuary. Her eyes widened at the size of the pipe organ and an amazing mosaic at the front. A sandal-footed, bearded shepherd stood nearly twenty feet tall with wooly lambs grazing at his feet. The beautiful artwork was made of bits of clear glass and was lighted from behind so that the mosaic took on an inner glow. The lapis-lazuli blue and ruby red that made up the man's garment glowed like gemstones, but the shepherd's eyes were the most amazing of all. They beamed benevolently out over the congregation with a peace and affection that Angela could hardly believe could be captured in bits of glass.

Fascinated by the artwork, her eyes began to follow the colorful banners that surrounded it. Phrases like "I am the Good Shepherd" and "Feed my lambs" leaped out at her. Intrigued, Angela shed her blasé, disinterested façade and began to listen to what was going on about her.

Voices swelled and soared in song. She was surprised to find one of the richest to be Rob's. He offered her a songbook with the words he had apparently memorized, but she could not keep her eyes on the page. Throughout the liturgy and message, her eyes traveled from face to face, resting briefly on each person's features.

As much as she fought it, Angela could not help but remember what she thought of as "the bushel basket and the light" conversation she had had with Rob. These people seemed to have an inner glow, much like the stained glass, backlit by the sun. Then it was not only Rob who possessed it. Could it be possible that Rob's fantastic theology did actually contain some grain of truth in it? *Surely not!* But the concept appealed to her. It was a warming thought to believe there was a Being who loved her for what she was at this very moment—and not what she was striving to become. The postlude began to reverberate through the aisles, preventing further musings.

Relieved to be escaping from her thoughts, Angela hustled down the long aisle toward the back of the church. The service over, everyone poured into the aisles, chattering. Dodging bodies, Angela led Rob and Kevin away from the visiting clusters, extricating herself from the crowd.

"Now, that wasn't so bad, was it?" Rob queried.

"The mosaic was beautiful," Angela admitted, "and I didn't realize you could sing."

"Oh, there's probably a lot about me you don't realize, Angela. But I'm willing to let you find out."

Kevin, eavesdropping behind them, let out a whoop. "Good line, Mr. Jordan. You're a smooth talker."

"And you, young man," Rob addressed him with mock ferocity, "had better learn to get lost when I'm hustling a lady!"

"You know, maybe you're all right, after all," Kevin observed kindly, bestowing hard-won approval on Rob.

Rob shot Angela a victorious look and said, "Just for that, I'll take you out for lunch—you pick the spot."

"McDonalds—where else?"

Rob glanced from Angela's hat into Kevin's eyes. "Are you sure about that? Maybe Miss Malone would like somewhere less casual."

"You *said* I could pick!"

"I did and I meant it. Do you mind, Angela?" Rob turned to her with a worried grin.

His gaze met one arched eyebrow. Doubtfully, she responded, "I suppose I could try it. If it means that much to Kevin."

"You mean you've never been to a McDonalds before?" Kevin stared at her in amazement.

"I've never been to any of those fast-food places. You're the first man I've ever known who offered."

"Brother, you've been going out with some duds!" Kevin observed.

Rob's head was nodding in sage agreement over the boy's shoulder.

Angela threw up her hands in disgust. "You wake me up; you drag me here; and now you criticize my dining habits! Who do you two think you are?"

"We are your guides to new experiences, Angela. Don't knock it. Church, fast food, and slow-pitch softball all in one day. How does that sound?" Rob took her elbow and guided her into the little car.

"Softball? I've never been to a softball game!" she balked.

"Our point exactly. This will be a day to remember, Angie."

Angela shot Rob a warning look, but he continued undaunted. "I can call you Angie today, can't I? It's so much—softer. Please?"

"I suppose. But remember—at work it's Angela." She was rewarded with a pleased grin. Rob had scored another coup. If his goal was to loosen up the stiff and proper Angela Malone, he was making great strides.

"You're gonna love it, Miss Malone. There's nothing like a good game of softball." Kevin's voice floated from the back of the Volkswagen where he was riding scrunched into a ball, his knees and shoulders vying for the same space.

Remembering the boy's presence, Angela tore her eyes from Rob's and slipped out of the front seat. Now that she'd gone this far with the day—she might as well see it to its completion.

Rob turned to her as they flocked through the restaurant doors with a family with five small children. "I think I'd better do the ordering. You can't get lobster newburg and petits fours here."

"Very funny. Even *I* knew that! But go ahead and order. Kevin and I will go hold a table."

Soon Rob returned, carrying a tray piled high with boxes, paper wrapped sandwiches, cups and paper scoopfuls of french fries.

"We'll never eat all that!" Angela protested. "Your eyes are bigger than your stomach."

"Don't count on it. You've forgotten that Kevin is a growing boy. This is just an appetizer for him."

"Right. Which of these things are mine?" Kevin unwrapped a burger and peeked under its top.

"Since Angela—Angie—had never been here before, I ordered one of everything. Give her a bite and let her pick what she wants. I think we can manage the rest.''

"Robert Jordan—you kook! *Nobody* orders one of everything on a menu!'' Angela gasped.

"Well, I just did. So eat hearty.''

Kevin was in such an unusually light-hearted and playful mood and Angela so enjoying the fare she had turned her nose up at for so long that their meal was nearly over before she realized how quiet Rob had been or how little he had eaten.

"Rob, are you okay? You've hardly said a word.''

He stretched in the molded plastic seat and slid his long legs from under the table. "I'm fine. Just couldn't get a word in edgewise with you two jabbering. Ready to go to the game?''

"You bet!'' Kevin jumped out of the seat and scooped up the tray and headed for the garbage can.

"He's loving every minute of this, Rob. He's like a new boy,'' Angela commented. "You're working miracles.''

"Hardly that. He's been hungry for attention. All I'm doing is giving him some—and so are you. Don't discount your company, lady lawyer. He needs us both.''

*And we both need you.* Angela left the words unspoken. It was difficult to express the gratitude she felt toward Rob. It was getting tangled up with some deeper emotions and she was afraid to dredge them up for fear of the consequences.

There was still a hesitation in his manner. He touched her so seldom, and when he did, it was as though he were handling fragile porcelain—with the utmost respect. At least Angela hoped it was respect and not disinterest. She had never been in a relationship that had developed in quite this manner.

Only ten minutes into the softball game, Kevin was pleading for a hot dog. Rob laughingly let him catch the vendor waving a foot-long bun in the air in front of the stands.

"He's going to be sick, Rob!"

"Nah. He'll be fine. I used to eat like that too. He's still growing."

"It seems to me you could use a little nourishment yourself today. You didn't eat very much at lunch. You look kind of pale, Rob. Do you feel all right?"

"Just fine. It's probably the bright sun. Quit worrying, Florence Nightingale."

Angela settled into the crook of his arm then, only vaguely aware of the activity on the field but acutely conscious of the rise and fall of Rob's chest with every breath. She was content to stay nestled there for the rest of the day. Only her mind wheeled with unanswered questions the morning's service had aroused.

But with every long hit or stolen base, Rob and Kevin would jump to their feet yelling encouragement, and Angela's little world would be disturbed. She would scarcely get settled against Rob's shoulder before something new happened on the field, and she would be displaced again.

All three were quiet as they rode the freeway toward the Simmons's mansion after the game. Kevin was obviously hesitant about going home; Angela was still remembering the feel of Rob's arm about her, and Rob's forehead was furrowed with unnamed thoughts.

After Angela escorted Kevin to the front door and deposited him with the grateful housekeeper, she returned to the Volkswagen to find Rob, eyes closed, resting his head on the back of the seat.

"Tired?"

"A continual state of existence for me lately, it seems. I can't seem to catch up—on my work, on my sleep, on anything."

"And that's exactly what Milton Simmons has in mind for you. As soon as that protective order is granted things will slow down."

"I hope so. Do you mind stopping by my office? I

want to pick up a few files to work on at home. It's still a mess from moving, but if I can clear a few things away it will help."

"Sure. I've been to three new places today. One more stop can't hurt."

A soft light gleamed in Rob's eyes as he spoke, "You've been a good sport, Angie. Thanks—from both Kevin and myself."

Angela felt a warm surge within her. Pleasing Rob Jordan was by far one of the most gratifying things she had ever done. It was with surprise that she looked up to see that they were already at his office. Three quick steps and they were inside.

"Rob! Look at this mess!"

"I know. I've been looking at it for several hours now. Any suggestions?" They surveyed the dingy room full of boxes and file cabinets. Two desks were heaped with files threatening to topple onto the floor.

"The first thing I'd do is get these files in a box before they become all mixed up. Can't you just stick them in a corner somewhere?"

"No those are my active files. They're the ones I need to be working on. I cleared out a bunch of them last night. But I think they must have started to reproduce when I turned the lights out."

Rob's attempt at a joke was ignored by Angela. "Did you come back here and work last night? How could you have? I was exhausted!"

"So was I. But I knew I'd never sleep thinking about all I had to do. Angie, were you serious about taking on a couple of clients until this Simmons thing is settled?"

Angela crossed the room to face him. She could tell how difficult it was for him to ask. "Very serious, Rob. Why don't you give me the files right now. I'll have my secretary set up appointments in the morning."

"Thanks, Angie. I don't know how I'll pay you

back, but I will. This Simmons thing has me stretched to the limit. . . ." Rob stumbled as he reached the desk, knocking his leg against a corner and causing an avalanche of papers to cascade onto the floor. He shook his head sharply to clear it and ran his palm across his forehead before stooping to retrieve the papers.

"Rob! What happened just now?"

"Nothing that a few hours sleep wouldn't cure."

"What is that supposed to mean? Are you getting sick?" Angela came to face him and ran an exploratory hand across his forehead. "Are you running a fever?"

"I'm all right. Just a little dizzy for a minute, that's all."

"Dizzy! You shouldn't be dizzy! Sit down, Rob. I don't like this one bit." Angela reached up and with her hands on his shoulders pushed him into a chair. Her alarm grew as she studied him. "You're white as a sheet. You're sick and not admitting it. I'm calling a doctor!"

"No! Don't do that!" The sharpness in Rob's tone stopped her. "I'm just tired, Angie. I've been this way for a few days. Everything will be fine once I get out from under this workload. Too much work, not enough sleep—that's all."

"And Kevin. You forgot to mention Kevin." Angela was becoming angry. "You're taking care of that boy like his father should be, while his father is out causing you trouble! It's not fair, Rob. It's just not fair."

Rob smiled wanly and ran his fingers through his hair. "But we'll keep battling all those injustices, Angie. You and I especially. It's our profession, after all." Then he shook his head as if trying to clear it.

Once again alarmed, Angela persisted, "Let me take you to see a doctor. Please."

"No, thanks. But maybe you could drive me home.

131

My head is spinning enough to make me a menace in traffic.''

"Just watch me. Are these the files you wanted me to take?'' Angela stuffed the folders under her arm and then helped Rob to his feet. He leaned on her for a moment, as if struggling for balance.

"I'm fine now. Let's go.'' They made their way to the car and Rob sank into the seat on the passenger side of the vehicle. He leaned back and closed his eyes, appearing very pale and quiet.

Angela turned the key in the ignition and the car spit into life. With a grinding of gears and a low chuckle from Rob, she sped into the traffic.

Angela kept one eye on the road and the other on her silent passenger. He had shut his eyes and appeared to be asleep. Taking matters into her own hands, Angela turned right at the next stoplight and steered the vehicle in the opposite direction from Rob's apartment.

Rob did not open his eyes until the car shuddered to a halt. They opened to unexpectedly bright light, but it was a moment before Angela saw that he realized where they were.

"Angela. I told you—''

"And I've told you lots of things, too. And you never listen. This time you're going to do something that I want.''

Rob sank back in the seat, too tired to argue, the light of the hospital emergency room sign gleaming on his cheek.

"Wait here. I'll go check you in.''

"Angie, I don't want to—''

"I know, I know. But if you're fine, I'll drive you home. If you're not, we should know about it.'' With that she jumped out of the car. As she reached the hood, she paused and turned back. Opening the door again, she pulled the keys from the ignition. "Just in case you should try to leave without me.'' She smiled and winked.

Rob groaned. "No wonder everyone says you have such a wonderful legal mind—it never quits working."

He had dozed off again by the time Angela and the emergency-room nurse returned with a wheelchair. It was easier to get a round peg into a square hole than to force Rob Jordan to ride in the contraption.

If looks could kill, Angela would have been lying dead in the street in front of the hospital. Rob, as balky as Angela had ever seen him, unwillingly gave the admissions nurse the information she needed.

"I'll get you for this," he muttered to Angela as a nurse wheeled him into an open room.

"Promise?" she responded, giving the top of his head a quick kiss before going to settle herself in the minuscule waiting room next door. Knotting and unknotting her fingers as she paced, Angela marked the minutes on the large white-faced clock across from her.

Nearly an hour passed before a white-coated physician, stepped into the cubbyhole with Angela.

"Miss Malone?"

"Yes?" Angela jumped up, her nerves taut as bow strings from the wait. She had recognized Rob's voice in the next room, but couldn't understand the muffled conversation. Fear was building within her that he'd be truly angry with her for bringing him here. But Rob was more likely to take care of others than himself. Someone had to watch out for him—and Angela was discovering more and more that she wanted to be the one to try.

"I'm Dr. Braun. I'd like to speak to you and Mr. Jordan together."

"Is he very angry?" Angela grimaced, apprehensive.

"Well, I don't know. But he shouldn't be. You did the right thing in bringing him. Whether he agrees or not. But we have to make some decisions on what happens next, and he'd like you to be there."

133

*At least he'll still speak to me,* Angela thought as she followed the doctor into the examining room.

Rob was sitting on the edge of the examining table, his arms bracing his upper body so he didn't tumble off onto the floor. His half-buttoned shirt hung outside of his trousers and he was very, very pale under the unflattering fluorescent lights.

"Rob, . . ." Angela began, feeling very timid after her bold decision to bring him here against his will.

"Come on. It's all right." Rob forgave her, holding out a hand.

"I know I shouldn't have, but I was so worried. . . ."

"Correction, Miss Malone. You should have brought him here, and I'm glad you did. This young man is suffering from various stress-related complaints—exhaustion and elevated blood pressure being not the least of them. He's got to rest—in a hospital or at home. I'd prefer to keep him here, but he seems inclined to disagree with me. Rather strongly, I might add."

Angela glanced at Rob and saw the concern in his eyes. Then it dawned on her. He probably didn't have medical insurance either! No wonder he had objected so strenuously.

"I think that it can be guaranteed that he will rest at home," Angela interjected. "If he doesn't, I'll pack him back in the car and bring him back. And now he knows I mean it."

A telling glance traveled between them. Angela was as determined as Rob, and she was in the position of power.

"Then I'll have a nurse give you written instructions and release Mr. Jordan. Please make an appointment to see me in one week. And if you've been following instructions, everything should be almost back to normal. If not, we may have to hospitalize you at that time. This episode should not be taken lightly. Good night."

"What did you get me into?" Rob chided.

"A week's rest. You should be thanking me."

"Thanking you for having to lie flat on my back in bed? *No* thanks!"

"You heard the doctor. You'd better behave or you'll end up here again next week. Consider this a reprieve with a chance to reform."

Just then a nurse bustled into the room with a complex sheet of written instructions that could be condensed into one word—rest. There was a food list limiting salt intake, cautions against stressful encounters and an appointment for the following week. Rob glanced at the paper with a doubtful look and then handed it to Angela.

"Here. You keep it. I don't like any part of it. All that's going to happen is that I'm going to fall farther and farther behind. And every time I think of Milton Simmons, I'm going to get a shot of stressful feelings anyway. And what about Kevin? I can't abandon him now!"

"Kevin can make himself useful. He can come by after school and make you supper. You can visit. You can play chess. All from your bed. It will be fine."

Angela received the withering look Rob shot her complacently. He was still speaking to her. That was all she asked.

Jumping lightly off the examining table, Rob stuffed his shirt back into his pants and buttoned the buttons.

"Let's get out of here."

"Okay. I'll drive."

"Then I'm not sure I want to go. Where are you planning to take me next?"

"Hop in the car and find out." After a tense few minutes at the cashier's desk, Rob met her in the car, waving away a nurse insisting again that he ride in a wheelchair.

"Hit it, driver. Get as far away from here and as fast as you can!" Rob's knuckles whitened as he gripped the dash.

He gave a sigh of relief as they pulled up in front of the apartment building. Angela parked and ran around to the passenger side to assist Rob from the car.

"Come on, I'll help you upstairs."

"I don't need any help, Angela. I'd been driving you around and opening your doors until you decided to drag me to the emergency room. Give me a break."

"I thought you'd enjoy having someone treat you like royalty," she retorted as she opened the apartment door. "Now, go get into bed and I'll call your parents."

"Oh, no, you don't! I'll take care of myself! My mother will come over here and smother me!"

"Rob, that's exactly what you need. I'm going to make us some hot chocolate while you get into bed. Then we'll discuss it. And, unless you can give me better reasons than that—I'm going to call your mother. Anyway, I'd like to meet her."

A groan emanated from the bedroom. "So that's what this is! A plot to meet my family. Why didn't you just ask? They would have had us over for dinner!"

Angela carried two mugs of steaming chocolate into the bedroom. Rob's clothes were tossed carelessly across a chair. He had found pajamas and crawled under a downy comforter on his bed. He was nearly asleep as Angela set the mugs down on the bedside stand.

"You're going to do it anyway, aren't you?" Rob's sleepy voice inquired.

"Do what?"

"Call my family."

"Probably."

"I'm going to have to figure out a better way to manage you," he muttered, and was asleep.

Thoughtfully Angela carried the two cool mugs back into Rob's kitchen. She would have to approach

Rob's parents carefully. They probably didn't know of her existence. To call them and tell them she had taken their son to the hospital might alarm them unduly. She would have to be very tactful.

Their phone number was written in Rob's bold script on the last page of the directory. He had made it very simple for her. Angela bit her lip nervously as the phone began to ring into the elder Jordan home.

"Jordan residence. Emily speaking."

Was Emily his mother? Was she a Jordan at all? How little she knew about this man of whom she had grown so fond! Finding her voice, Angela spoke.

"This is Angela Malone. I'm a friend of Rob's. I'd like to speak to his mother, please."

"This is Rob's mother. What can I do for you, Angela?" The voice was well-modulated and pleasant. Angela breathed a sigh of relief.

"I just wanted to call and tell you that Rob isn't feeling well. I—"

"Rob? Not well? What's wrong?" The voice betrayed alarm.

"Please, don't worry. Rob didn't want to tell you, but I thought you should know. I took him to see a doctor. It's exhaustion mostly. Rob's resting now."

"I'll be right over. Stay where you are. I want to meet you, Miss Malone." The next thing Angela heard was the persistent buzz of a dial tone.

What had she gotten herself into now?

## CHAPTER 9

A SOFT TAPPING ON THE DOOR signaled the arrival of
Mrs. Jordan. Nervously, Angela slipped into the
shoes she had discarded and went to open it. Before
her stood a statuesque woman wearing a sable throw
about her shoulders. Mrs. Jordan sailed through the
door and tossed the fur cape casually across a chair.
Then she turned to Angela.

"Now, where is Rob, and what's wrong with him?
It wouldn't surprise me one bit if it were malnutrition.
He doesn't take care of himself like he should. He'll
find a stray to feed and forget about himself!"

Angela smiled. Rob's mother knew him rather well.

"You're on the right track, but it's exhaustion, not
malnutrition."

"I should have guessed! He's got some big case
he's been working on that has him on the go at all
hours. And how do you fit into all of this?" Angela
found another pair of firmament blue eyes boring into
hers.

Startled by the sudden switch in topics, Angela took
a moment to gather her wits before answering. How

*did* she fit in? That was a question to which she, too, would like an answer.

"I'm a friend of Rob's. I'm also an attorney. We met in court. He's been helping me with a problem, and I want to return the favor. I'm afraid he's going to be very angry with me in the morning. I took him to the emergency room without his consent. But he looked terrible, and the doctor said I did the right thing. Anyway, here I am. Rob's asleep. I thought I should let you know. He wasn't very happy about that either, I'm afraid."

"You're very pretty, my dear. I doubt that Rob could stay angry with you very long even if he wanted to. And please don't feel badly about admitting that Rob didn't want you to call me. He accuses me regularly of overmothering. He knew I'd see this as the ideal opportunity for plying my trade!"

The two laughed together, and a bond was instantly spawned between them. They loved the same man, and the fact gave them a common meeting ground.

"Speaking of trades, you do very lovely work as a decorator. I've seen two suites of furniture in here since I met Rob and they have been exquisite."

"Thank you. Fortunately for me, Rob doesn't care if he's sitting on a Queen Anne chair or an orange crate. I'm afraid I take advantage of his home and my own for trying things out. He calls it 'free warehousing,' and he's probably right. Furniture does tend to come and go in our family."

"Do you work out of your home?" Angela struggled to grasp the odd situation.

"Yes. And I like to have certain items on hand for my clients—just so they can visualize what I'm planning for their homes. It works rather well—or at least it will until my son puts his foot down. He's quite disinterested in material things as you must know by now, so he puts up with my idiosyncrasies."

Emily Jordan kicked off her shoes and joined

Angela on the couch. "Now, tell me about yourself. Have you lived in Chicago long?"

"All my life. I did go to boarding schools out East as a high-school student, but I was anxious to get back home."

Emily nodded in agreement. "Rob has always loved it here. We considered moving when he was a boy, but we didn't want to tear him away from his friends."

Angela smiled, considering Rob as a child. Emily Jordan seemed to read her very thoughts. "He was a beautiful child—physically adept from the first. His hair was nearly white as a toddler, but darkened to the color of wheat by the time he was a teen. His eyes seemed to get bluer as his hair got darker. A nice combination, I've always thought." Then Emily blushed slightly and went on to explain herself, "He looks very much like his father. Perhaps I'm partial to sandy-haired, blue-eyed men."

*Perhaps I am, too.*

Angela liked Rob's mother very much; she was frank and matter-of-fact. Angela felt as though she had known Mrs. Jordan for many years.

Then his mother asked the question that cut to the very quick of the issue. "Angela, can you accept Rob's faith?"

"I don't know, Mrs. Jordan. I'm still trying to understand it. It seems a rather shaky premise on which to build a life—so much faith and so little fact."

The older woman nodded sympathetically. "I know what you mean. Rob came to believe as he does after he left home. It's been a long journey for us to see things his way. But Rob is a very convincing witness."

*The bushel basket and the light. A light by its very nature must shine.*

"You have a great deal of respect for your son, don't you?" Angela commented.

"Yes. Rob's taken the hard road when an easier one has always been available to him. I suppose you knew he worked for Smith, Keyes and Lovall before he struck out on his own?"

Angela nodded. Perhaps now she would find an answer to some of the questions she had been asking about Rob Jordan.

"He earned a great deal of money with that firm. He's a very good attorney, they say. But he felt called to do what he's doing instead. Serving others. Going where he's needed. It took his father and me a long time to accept that. We wanted a wealthy son in a prestigious law firm. Instead we got this." Mrs. Jordan waved a hand toward a crack in the wall.

Angela smiled with compassion.

"So how did you come to accept it, Mrs. Jordan? I'm not sure I could have done it in your place."

"Couldn't you, my dear?" Emily Jordan studied Angela with that all-knowing X-ray expression Rob so often used.

"Well, there *is* an . . . aura . . . about Rob that's very endearing . . . and perhaps I *am* too fond of material things. They're very important to me. But," Angela was suddenly indignant, "after all, *I've earned them!*"

Emily only smiled understandingly.

Angela was chagrined to find herself so irrationally defensive. Who was she trying to convince anyway?

"Rob's lifestyle forced us to reevaluate our lives, Angela, to straighten out our priorities." Emily Jordan began placidly, "We've begun to go to church again after a very long vacation. Somehow Rob has been able to make us desire what *he* has. Ironic, isn't it, when he appears to have so little on the surface? Then, perhaps you didn't want a serious discussion. I'm sorry—have I burdened you with things you didn't want to hear?"

"Not at all. Rob has that effect on people. He

makes them question their values. I don't know how it happens but it's part of his charm!"

"Then you *do* understand!" Emily exclaimed delightedly. "And I'm so happy you were here to put my errant son in his place. Should I go in and check on him, or will I only wake him up?"

"I don't think an earthquake would wake him tonight. The doctor gave him something to make him sleep."

"Well, I'll stay until morning. He'll be furious when he wakes up and finds me here. I hope he has the ingredients for waffles—that will make him forgive me for spending the night!" Emily cheerfully settled herself deeper into the couch.

Angela grinned as she left Rob's apartment. He was in good hands. His physical health should improve rapidly—if the women in his life didn't drive him crazy first!

The next morning Angela sat at her desk in a thoughtful mood. Thoughts of Rob had interrupted her sleep and things he had said and done nagged at her conscience. Whatever fired that light of Rob's certainly had a powerful effect on people! It had caused her to agree to see the motley group of Rob's clients whose files were piled on her desk. Angela's secretary had been set to the task of phoning them and making appointments. But what would the receptionist at Henshaw, Radison and Grimes think when Angela's new clients started filing in?

By two o'clock the first of Rob's clients had arrived.

"Miss Malone. Mr. Fowler is here to see you. Do you want me to send him in?" Angela heard an unsure note in the receptionist's voice. Whoever this Mr. Fowler was, he had managed to rattle the stoic Ms. Payne.

"Please, Ms. Payne."

Shortly the door to her office edged open and the brim of a battered hat appeared. After a brief pause, brown eyes in a dark, leathery face entered. At Angela's welcoming wave, the face broke into a toothless grin and a small man inched his way into the intimidating recesses of her office.

Suddenly remembering his manners, he swept the well-worn headgear into his hands, curling the rim in agitated fingers.

"Mr. Fowler."

"*Si*, I mean, yes, I am Mr. Rico Fowler. The lady at the desk say I should come in." His eyes darted about the room, growing wide with awe. The man, obviously a Mexican-American, seemed never to have seen such luxury before.

Angela rose from her mahogany desk and slipped from behind it to shake her newest client's slightly grubby hand.

"I am Angela Malone. I appreciate your coming in today on such short notice, but I am temporarily taking care of a few of Mr. Jordan's clients and I had a free slot in my appointment book."

"Has Mr. Rob gone away? I am frightened when he cannot see me. He is sick? No?"

"Mr. Rob, uh, Mr. Jordan is resting. He's been working very hard lately, and the doctor told him to take the week off. And I am helping out so he can do just that." Seeing the alarm in the little man's eyes, Angela hastened to continue, "Mr. Jordan will be fine. Please don't worry. I assure you that he'll be back at work in just a few days."

Relief spread over Fowler's face. "Good! Mr. Rob is a wonderful man. It would break my heart if he were very ill."

Angela stared at the man in amazement. She believed it actually *would* break the little fellow's heart if something happened to Rob. What client of hers would notice if she were missing? None that she

143

could think of—unless she dropped in a heap in front of them. Quashing the idle introspection, she steered the conversation toward the purpose for Fowler's visit.

"What can I do for you? Since Rob is your regular attorney, I'm afraid you'll have to acquaint me with your entire case." Angela settled into her leather chair with Fowler's meager file. He hadn't had many legal problems of note by the looks of it.

"It's my car, Mees Malone. The car I bought that I don't want."

"Please go on." Already Angela didn't like the sound of it.

"I've been saving for a very long time to buy a car. And I finally found her—a beautiful 1973 Pontiac that I could afford. I paid three hundred dollars and signed a paper saying I would pay one hundred dollars a month for a year."

"It must be some car," Angela thought to herself, remembering the new Porsche she'd been admiring only last week and the monthly payments she and the salesman had discussed.

"Well," the little fellow continued, "I drove it home to show my brother-in-law. He's a mechanic, Mees Malone, at an uptown garage."

Angela gritted her teeth and tolerated Mr. Fowler's forays in family history.

"Rodrigo, that's my brother-in-law, took it for a drive. When he returned he had a very unhappy look on his face. He said I'd been cheated. He said the car dealer had put something . . . ," the small man struggled for the word, ". . . additives in the oil to hide that the engine needed a major overhaul. I didn't believe him, but a few days later my car started to burn blue smoke. Rodrigo says that my new car is no good, Mees Malone. I want my money back!"

Fowler was so distressed, Angela was afraid he would break into tears. Gently she prodded him for answers.

"Do you remember what you signed?"

"*Si*. Lots of papers. But I don't read much, Mees Malone. They told me it was all right not to read them. So I just signed my name."

Angela winced. "Did they tell you anything the papers said, or did they give you copies?"

"They said I was buying the car 'as is' but I thought that was okay. How else would you buy a car but as it is? I think these are bad men and that they tricked me, Mees Malone! Crooked men! And I told them so!"

"You've talked to them again?"

"*Si*. I went to ask for my money back. My car is huffing and puffing smoke. People point and laugh. I can't drive a car like that! It costs too much for oil."

"And what did they tell you when you requested that they return your money?"

"They said, 'You bought it. You pay for it.' They said they would take my car away if I don't! Why should I have to pay for something that doesn't work?"

*Why, indeed?* Angela left the words unspoken. Injustice ran rampant at every level of society, apparently, but this was unconscionable!

Fowler pulled a crumpled letter from his breast pocket. "This came in the mail. My brother-in-law read it to me and told me that I must make the first payment within seven days or they will come and take my car away and sell it to someone else, but that I would still have to pay for it."

Suddenly his shoulders sagged under the weight of his mental and financial burden. "They took my car, Mees Malone. Now I have nothing."

"Are you sure it wasn't stolen?"

"*Si*. I called the dealership, and they said that they had taken it in the night. And that I would have to pay for that too."

Anger surged through Angela. The poor fellow had sacrificed to get that car and been duped in the process. Her fingers snapped to life and she began jotting notes on a yellow legal pad.

"Mr. Fowler, the first step is to sue the car dealership, seeking full restitution and to obtain a temporary restraining order to prevent said dealership from disposing of the vehicle or altering it in any way during the pendency of the action. I will take those steps immediately."

Angela looked up at her client and was met by round brown eyes filled with awe and bewilderment.

"Did you understand what I just said, Mr. Fowler?"

The dark head shook in something akin to wonder. "No, Mees Malone, but it sounded wonderful. Just like Mr. Rob sometimes talks."

Angela stifled a grin and started over. "I'm going to try to stop them from doing anything to the car to fix or change it until this matter is settled. Also, I am going to sue the car dealership to try to get your money back and prevent you from having to pay any more. How does that sound?"

"You are as good as Mr. Rob! Thank you! Thank you!" Delight spread across the leathered face.

"Well, let's hope so, Mr. Fowler. Leave your address with my secretary, and I'll be in touch."

Fowler nodded, bowed and uttered his gratitude all the way out the door to Angela's office. Angela shook her head and sank into the cushiony client's chair he had just vacated.

Then the impact of what she had just done struck her. She had just committed at least four thousand dollars worth of legal services to a claim worth less that fifteen hundred! And what would she receive? She couldn't bill the man more than fifty dollars. He would never be able to pay it back. It was no wonder Rob had holes in his shoes. He must have them in his head as well to do work like this!

"Still," she thought as she returned to the papers

behind her desk, "it was a grand feeling to help the man." Although if she assessed it, she wasn't sure the feeling would add up to four thousand dollars worth of pleasure. . . .

"Sprucing up your clientele, Angela?" Pete's sarcastic question floated through the open door.

"You'd better come in and explain yourself, mister," Angela retorted, already cognizant of what was coming—Mr. Henshaw had given her a very odd stare in the hall earlier.

"You know what I mean. That filthy little man who had an appointment with you this afternoon! Really, Angela! Has business fallen off that much?"

"Everyone has a right to legal representation, Pete. Mr. Fowler is no exception."

"But *here?* Isn't this a rather elite establishment for his type? Whatever happened to Legal Aid? Services are free there."

*They are here, too, buddy—at least for the duration of Rob's illness.*

"Well, aren't you going to explain?"

"There's nothing to explain, Pete. I've decided to take on Mr. Fowler as a client. I was recommended by his former attorney—just for now."

"Thank goodness for that! You'll ruin the whole atmosphere of the office with his type running in and out!" Pete gave a theatrical shudder.

"Pete, suddenly I'm very tired. Of you. Good day."

Pete raised one surprised eyebrow. Angela knew she had him baffled. She had shed a portion of the snobbery she had formerly cultivated. Rob's open acceptance of everyone he met was rubbing off on her. She was beginning to regret her former lofty and condescending behavior.

*Ruining the atmosphere of the office, humph!*

Time sped by as Angela prepared the foundation of Mr. Fowler's legal case. Curious about the reputation

147

of the car dealership, she made several illuminating phone calls. Finally she determined to use extensive pretrial discovery tactics to find out exactly where Used Cars, Inc. stood.

*An expensive decision, Malone,* she thought to herself. Interrogatories, depositions, requests for the production of documents and admissions were steep, but she felt compelled to go ahead. She had promised.

Exhausted by the problem that lay before her, Angela began to thumb through a stray file on her desk. Before her eyes appeared a photocopied page in a bold, easily recognizable hand. Rob's notes on the Hannah Green case.

Angela blushed deep crimson in the solitude of her office. Her intentions had been far from honorable when she had lifted these notes from Rob. She knew in her heart she had planned to use them to subvert his defense.

Ashamed and repentant, she tore it to shreds and began to thumb through the journal before her.

When her eyes were too scratchy to read any further, Angela put down her book and glanced at her watch. *Six-thirty. Dinnertime. Rob.*

Jumping from her desk, she then scooped her small leather handbag from the top drawer and headed for the parking lot. She had more responsibilities than Mr. Fowler to attend to.


Voices and pleasant smells drifted from Rob's apartment as Angela stood before the door. Unaccountably shy, she had to muster the courage to knock.

"Come on in. It's open."

She pushed at the door and stepped inside. Before her stood Kevin, an apron across his middle, a spatula in one hand and a woebegone look on his face.

"Pinch me please, I must be dreaming."

"Very funny, Ms. Malone. You're just in time. I

think you saved Mr. Jordan from a fate worse than death."

"Your cooking?"

"Right." The spatula fell to the floor with a clatter as Kevin pulled the apron over his head.

Picking up the utensil, Angela queried, "And what is on the menu for this evening, Gourmet Gus?"

"Grilled cheese sandwiches and tomato soup. I've got the soup figured out, but Mr. Jordan says to butter the *outsides* of the sandwiches!"

"The reserves are here, so take off your apron. I'll go say hello to Rob and then finish supper. Perhaps you can keep him company while I'm in the kitchen."

"I'm not much company." Kevin dropped his head.

"Rob and I don't agree with that. Come on. Let's go say hello." She feigned a swing with the spatula as the boy trotted toward Rob's room.

Angela peeked around the corner of the bedroom door. Rob lay sleeping in a tangled ball of sheets and blankets. His sandy hair curled on the pillow beneath him and one arm was flung out over his head. He looked very vulnerable. And very handsome.

At their footsteps, Rob stirred. Tossing in the rumpled bed, his eyes met Angela's and widened slightly in pleasure before he began to rub them with balled fists.

"Hi, lady lawyer."

"Hi, yourself. Feeling better?"

"Much. I haven't slept like this since I was six years old."

"You still look about six. Notice the jumble you made of this bed."

"I can't remember needing a shave when I was six."

"Some things do change. Get out of that bed. You can shave and Kevin and I will straighten it out. Then I'll finish the dinner Kevin started and we can eat."

Rob's eyes lighted in surprise as he glanced at the boy. "You made dinner? Really? I thought you were only kidding!"

"Well, I sort of started to. Ms. Malone came just in time to bail me out."

"Good boy. Excuse me while I get cleaned up." Rob shuffled sleepily toward the bathroom, rubbing his head with both hands, stirring his hair into a spiky, disheveled mess. Angela and Kevin smiled behind his back in affectionate camaraderie.

By the time Angela had buttered the outside of the sandwiches and grilled them in a frying pan, Kevin had set the table with the mismatched utensils Rob owned. Rob, freshly showered and shaved, came to the table with loudly voiced accolades.

"This is great! Angela, if things go bad for you in the legal business, maybe you and Kevin can start a catering service!" Rob teased as he sat down.

"I may have to yet," Angela thought, remembering the expensive suit she had set in motion for Mr. Fowler and Pete's cutting remarks.

Aloud, she said, "You seem much better tonight."

"I should be. I've slept like a bear in hibernation. I thought maybe I'd do a little work this evening. . . ."

"Oh, no, you don't!" Kevin and Angela chimed in unison.

Rob put his hands before his face, palms outward in mock fear. "Okay, okay. I give up. When you two are getting along you make a mean team."

Kevin and Angela grasped each other's hands across the table in a victory handshake and Rob stretched for a sandwich. Before he took a bite he laid it on his plate and bowed his head for a moment. Angela and Kevin watched him warily and wide-eyed, but he didn't speak. When he raised his head, Rob asked, "Where's the soup?" Relieved that the awkward moment was past, Angela nearly toppled her chair in her haste to get the pan from the kitchen. Would she ever get used to Rob's ways?

After the few dishes were washed, the three of them sat in the living room on Emily Jordan's exquisite furniture and carried on a desultory conversation. Angela curled up next to Rob on a love seat and Kevin lounged across from them on the large couch.

"I'm glad you came over after school, Kevin," Rob commented, his forefinger winding a curl in Angela's raven hair.

"It's more peaceful over here. My dad's not barking down my neck, at least."

"Does he do that a lot?"

"It's pretty good when just my mom is around. But she's scared of my dad, so she won't stick up for me."

"What is he after you about, Kevin?" Rob inquired.

"School, grades, how I look, how I act—everything."

"Does anything you do please him?"

"Not that I know of. And believe it or not, I've really tried. Finally I just gave up. I'd try some more if I thought it would help."

Angela's heart went out to the boy. Rob was right after all. Maybe there was hope for Kevin. She snuggled closer to Rob, overjoyed that he had not let her give up too easily.

Soon she felt Rob's breathing slow and deepen. She turned to look at him. Asleep. She and Kevin exchanged a smile before they cajoled their sleepy charge back to bed. Then quietly the two of them turned off the lights and left the apartment.

Pete was gloating when Angela arrived at the office the next morning.

"Did you hear the news? Hannah Green's attorney had to file a motion for a protective order. He can't keep up!" Pete chuckled gleefully. "Simmons will have him where he wants him in no time now. I'm glad I'm not the one battling Milton Simmons!"

*If you only knew, Pete, if you only knew*, Angela thought to herself. What coffee room conversation it would make if anyone knew that Rob Jordan was flat on his back in bed, and the son of his arch rival was coming in after school to cook his supper! What if they knew that Rob had been teaching Milton Simmons's son chess and guitar?

But Rob was looking stronger and leaner after his much needed rest. If he could just hang on a few more days! His case documentation for Hannah's case was flawless. She felt sure he could put Simmons in his place if things didn't move too quickly.

And Angela had problems of her own. She had opened a real hornet's nest in the Fowler case. The more she learned, the more appalled she became. She had become convinced that the car dealership took advantage of its customers quite regularly, exploiting those of limited resources. It would be simple because of the nature of what they were selling—used cars—and their impoverished clientele.

It was midafternoon before Angela realized she hadn't taken time for lunch and this was the day of Rob's doctor appointment. She dialed his number with the blunt end of her pencil, preserving the glossy lacquer on her nails.

"Hello."

"Rob, this is Angela."

"Hi, lady lawyer. To what do I owe this great pleasure?"

"You have a clinic appointment this afternoon. You had planned to go, hadn't you?"

"Oh, I suppose. Did you leave that appointment card somewhere?"

"On the sofa table, propped against a lamp. You weren't going to go, were you?" she accused.

"No, not really. . . ."

"I'll be right over. We'll have plenty of time to make it if I leave the office now."

"Angela, you don't have to bother. . . ."

"No bother. See you." With that, she deliberately dropped the receiver into its cradle. She had suspected he would try to forget that appointment.

"You don't trust me, do you?" were Rob's accusatory words of greeting. He looked wonderful standing in the sunlight in front of his apartment, glaring into her car.

"Not a bit. Hop in."

Angela seldom saw him in casual clothes. They suited him. He wore chocolate-brown shirt and pants and an ivory sweater swung casually over one shoulder. The few pounds he had shed gave him a lean, athletic look. His hair needed a trim, and it curled in his collar.

*Gorgeous, absolutely gorgeous*, Angela thought as he climbed into her car. The irritated look he shot her made her heart quiver. Perhaps he didn't want her mothering after all. Yet it was so difficult to stay away.

But it was a forgiving smile he bestowed on her as he entered the doctor's office. She breathed a sigh as he winked before closing the door behind him. It seemed eons until it opened again.

"Well, Mr. Jordan. It seems you've had some good nursing over the past week." The doctor stepped into the hallway and met Angela's eyes as he spoke.

"Not bad, considering how difficult it is to get good help these days," Rob bantered.

"But remember, this was just a warning. Don't get yourself into the same kind of bind again. You can't keep snapping back from this kind of thing forever. Slow down, son."

Rob nodded amiably and took Angela's elbow. As he steered her down the corridor, he whispered in her ear, "There, are you satisfied?"

Angela grinned and nodded.

"Now I have a surprise for you." Rob grinned.

"Really? What could it be?"

"I suppose you're sure it's not a mink coat or a quart of Chanel No. 5?"

"Never occurred to me."

"My mother has invited you to dinner tonight. Would you like to come?"

Would she? Angela was eager to solve this puzzle that was Rob Jordan. Perhaps a visit to his home would provide her with some more pieces.

"I'd love to. What time?"

"Eight. Since I got a clean bill of health, may I pick you up? I'm not an invalid any more."

"I'll be ready at seven-thirty. Is dinner at your house formal?"

"Who knows? It all depends on what furniture Mother has in the dining room. Just keep your fingers crossed that it's not Japanese. We'll end up sitting on the floor."

Laughter burbled into Angela's throat. Maybe visiting the elder Jordans wouldn't answer any questions, but it would no doubt be fun.

## CHAPTER 10

"YOU GREW UP *HERE?*" Angela's astonishment flourished as Rob drove through the wrought-iron arches that set his parents' home apart from the others on the winding street.

"Yeah. Terrible, isn't it?"

"It's absolutely one of the most magnificent houses I've ever seen! What do you mean, 'terrible?' " She eyed the massive Tudor with something akin to awe. Turrets peaked and tiny leaded-glass windows glimmered. It was like a fairy-tale castle.

"The waste. Three families could raise their children in the house instead of one. It's embarrassing, really, but what can I do?"

Angela stared at the man next to her. Embarrassing? This was what she lusted for in life—a beautiful home in an elite section of the city. How could anyone who lived and worked in a slum find this place embarrassing? Maybe it *was* impossible for her to understand Rob Jordan after all. Then she caught the flash of his teeth in the fading light.

"Rob," she began hesitantly, "are you teasing me or . . . did you *mean* what you just said?"

His growling chuckle crescendoed. "Perhaps I was being a little dramatic to make a point. It's a great house. I do love it here. It just seems so extravagant when others are struggling to put a roof over their heads."

"It's not a very new home, is it?" she commented as they made their way up to the imposing front door.

"No. My grandfather was in railroads. He built it for my grandmother only ten years before they died. Mom and Dad moved in when I was small. Mother went berserk over the possibilities for her interior-decorating business. She still has an office downtown because this area is not zoned for business. But it's become quite a coup for customers to be invited to Emily Jordan's for tea once they've hired her. More than once, Mother has sold the furnishings of the entire first floor of the house 'as is' to a wealthy customer."

"I can see why. I'd take it in a minute." Angela peered through the tiny panes of glass flanking the wooden door.

She could hear the amusement in Rob's voice as he added. "The 'less promising' customers are steered toward my apartment. If mother could get me to water her potted palms and keep a maid, she might trust me with some of her 'better' pieces. I attempt to be derelict about the apartment to avoid that at all possible costs. I have enough difficulty as it is explaining to the landlord why moving vans visit me so regularly."

Just as Angela lifted a hand to ring the bell, Rob stopped her. "No! Don't ring the bell! There's only one servant. She'll be run ragged in the kitchen right now. Let's not bother her." Rob threw open the door and stepped inside. "Anybody home?"

"Rob, darling! Why didn't you ring? Hello, Angela. It's so nice to see you again. Come inside."

Emily Jordan, in an outrageously arty batik caftan, billowed toward them.

156

"Rob, you're looking peaked. Did you take the vitamins I left for you?"

"Mother, you're looking like a balloon. Where did you get that dress?"

"Touché!" Emily turned toward Angela. "He gets so independent sometimes. I think it's rather cute."

Angela stifled a laugh as Rob rolled his eyes behind his mother. Their affection was apparent—and so were their divergent personalities.

Rob shrugged out of his sweater and hung the shawl Angela handed him in the closet. Then, turning and taking each lady by an elbow, he steered them into the living room.

A massive fireplace rose floor to ceiling before her. Built-in bookcases flanked the fieldstone monument. Before the fire in a leather wing chair sat Rob's carbon copy, reading the evening paper.

"Carl, the kids are here," Emily announced, warming Angela's heart with her open acceptance as one of the "kids."

"Oh, hi! Didn't hear you ring or see the maid fly by. Good to see you. Welcome!"

Rob's sandy-haired, wholesome good looks had been passed directly from father to son. But for a plethora of smile lines around the eyes and about fifteen extra pounds, this man could have been Rob's twin.

"I'm pleased to meet you, Mr. Jordan. I was just noticing the amazing resemblance between you and your son."

"Curse of the Jordans, we call it. Blatantly wholesome. Disgusting. It's a good thing my father was in railroads instead of gambling. Our features would never do—too honest. Rob's got it worse than I have, but I suspect he cultivates it. Maybe I should start if it attracts pretty girls like you."

Delighted and dumfounded by the monologue, Angela did something she thought she had conquered as a teenager. She giggled. And giggled. And giggled. Until Emily Jordan began to laugh as well. Rob, baffled by the two women, began to chuckle. His father, amazed at the response he had wrought, joined in. It was several minutes before the hilarity subsided.

Wiping the merry tears from her eyes, Angela apologized. "I'm so sorry, but that struck me funny. I'm usually much better behaved at dinner parties!"

"Well, no matter what else you do tonight, you have free rein. You've managed to make an old man feel witty," Carl Jordan responded. "Now come to dinner. I see the maid waving the 'eat it now or I resign' flag in the kitchen. And by the way, Rob, Kim called just before you arrived. Apparently there's no hurry in returning the call."

Rob nodded briefly. Angela noticed the faint smile that pulled at his lips at the name, but her curiosity was diverted by the lavish dinner Emily Jordan had concocted.

The meal was exquisite. Mineral water glistened in crystal goblets. Tiny crystal salt cellars stood at each place setting and the maid bustled to each of them offering to grind pepper onto their salads.

"This salad dressing is magnificent, Emily! It's so different! Tell me, what's in it?" Angela noticed Rob suddenly eyeing the greens with suspicion.

"Rose petals—believe it or not! I learned the secret from one of my clients. Rose petals! Do you really like it?"

"Rose petals!" Rob exclaimed. "Mother, you promised!"

"I promised a lovely meal. You're enjoying it, aren't you, Angela?"

"Very much. What's wrong with you, Rob?"

"I asked for a regular meal—like meat loaf, mashed potatoes, gravy. I specifically said no weird experiments. I knew I couldn't trust you, Mother."

Emily smiled patiently at her son. "Now, dear, your life would be so dull without me."

Finally Carl Jordan chimed in. "Just be glad you don't live with her anymore, Rob. I have to eat all these concoctions by myself now. I've often thought that your moving out and leaving me alone with your mother constituted parental abuse. What do you have to say about that, Angela?"

On the spot, Angela battled the giggles once again. This was the craziest, most endearing family she had ever met. "Well, I rather like the dressing. My compliment was sincere. But my question is, where did you get the recipe?"

"One of my clients is writing a book on cooking with flowers. She gave me several to try. I thought it would be fun if we had some of them tonight. I added a few nasturtiums, the blossoms mostly, to the salad. And I seasoned the roast chicken with lavender. It smelled divine while it was cooking!"

Rob slumped in his seat. "Do you have any peanut butter and jelly in the kitchen, or do you just snack in the flower beds these days?"

"Don't be difficult, Rob. You can't eat every flower. Just a select few. I'll give my recipes to Angela. And don't make such fun—you've eaten the flowers of herbs such as oregano, chives, and basil all your life!"

Rob straightened in his chair and winked at Angela. "You wanted to know about my family? Now you know. And you can understand why I prefer to keep them a secret. We have no other skeletons in our closet though. Mother ground them up for calcium!"

The playful repartee lasted all evening and it was with sadness that Angela saw it come to an end.

"I suppose we should be going. I have a week's worth of mail to wade through. Angela refused to bring it to me."

"Good for her. We're glad Rob found you, Angela." Angela clutched Emily Jordan's hand in mute gratitude. How fond she had become of these people.

Back in the confines of the rusty Volkswagen, Angela studied Rob's features in the ethereal glow from the dashboard. Her visit to his family had only created questions, not answered them. It was obvious that Rob had become accustomed to beans after living on a caviar budget. The need to acquire that drove her to her own frenetic lifestyle was completely lacking in Rob's nature. She had begun to desire that peaceful acceptance for her own life—whatever the cost.

The car grumbled to a halt in front of Angela's building.

"Do you want to come inside?"

"Yes. But I won't. Get plenty of rest—doctor's orders, you know."

"Well, I'm glad you're listening. And thank you, Rob, for a wonderful evening. I've never laughed so much."

"'Prim and Proper Sophisticate, Angela Malone, Lets Hair Down'—good headline material. I'm pleased to see you laugh. You take yourself too seriously, Angela." Rob's voice softened as he spoke, and his head lowered toward hers until their noses touched. He gently rubbed the tip of her nose with his own, and Angela heard him mutter, "I'll never know what the Eskimos see in it," before his lips came down hard and passionately on hers, wiping every thought from her mind.

Senses still reeling, she clasped her hands at the back of his neck and pulled him toward her, hungry for his touch. His hand followed the nape of her neck causing shivers to dance in her spine. Every nerve came alive as she felt his body pressing toward hers, and disappointment surged through her when he pulled away.

"Too much of that, and my blood pressure will get out of hand again." He smiled, his finger trailing a path around her lips. For the first time that evening Angela noticed how tired his eyes seemed.

Feeling guilty for being so selfish, she pushed him away from her, burying the palms of her hands and the tips of her fingers into the warm fabric that stretched across his chest. She could feel the steady beat of his heart thumping against the heel of one hand. "Go get some sleep."

"I think I'd better. But how about going to the Indiana Dunes State Park with me on Saturday?"

"It's been years since I've been there! Is it still a tourist spot?"

"As far as I know. Pack a picnic lunch. We'll find a spot to eat on the way. I'll need a break by then."

"Okay. Sleep well." Angela slipped from the car. Rob waited until she was through the security lock before he pulled away.

Angela was smiling as she stepped into her apartment. An entire day with Rob Jordan—just what the doctor ordered.

Angela was up before seven on Saturday, boiling potatoes and eggs for salad, browning chicken in her little-used electric frying pan, and packing utensils into the marvelous wicker basket she had purchased just for the day.

"Rob would just die if he knew how much I spent on this meal," she chatted to herself as she arranged a red-and-white-checked tablecloth and napkins in the bottom of the basket and piled it with bright red plastic plates and cups.

She had made some other purchases as well. Stretched tightly across her narrow hips was a pair of denim jeans, the first she had owned since she was a child. Even with the bold designer name tattooed on the back pocket, she felt rather shabby and underdressed. It was quite a comedown for a woman who lounged in silk pajamas and robes with ostrich boas. But Rob would like it. And today, that was what counted.

She was waiting on the front step when the little Volkswagen sputtered into view.

"Good morning!" Rob jumped from the car to relieve her of the gigantic basket. "Did I mention that we'd be back this evening? There's enough in here for a month!"

"Recipes containing flowers seem to weigh more than ordinary, run-of-the-mill foods."

Rob feigned horror and let the basket plummet toward the concrete before he grinned and halted the descent. "If there is so much as a daisy on the napkins it will be too much for me!"

"You're safe. I've decided to leave anything quite that gourmet to your mother."

"Leave it to Mother, all right. She'll always come up with something new. They liked you very much, you know. You made a hit."

Pleased, Angela responded, "And I liked them. Now I know where you get your looks and your sense of humor. Although you're still very different from your parents."

"I work at it," Rob grinned. Then his gaze turned subtly into a leer. "Blue jeans! Honest-to-goodness blue jeans! Am I looking at Angela Malone, society lawyer, or do my eyes deceive me?"

"Stifle it, Jordan. I thought they were appropriate for the day."

"I didn't know you had a practical bone in your body, Angela. It's great. I'm still learning things about you. Let's go."

As they drove through the streets of Chicago, Angela studied Rob's sturdy profile and thought, *And there's still something very important that I need to know about you.*

As in each and every visit Angela had made to the Indiana dunes, they startled her. The golden white dunes rose to greet them and sent sand drifting across

162

the road in a gusty wind. To find the rising hills on the shores of Lake Michigan instead of on a windy gulf shore was a continual surprise. Sea gulls were dipping from the sky, gliding near the ground, and soaring again in an age-old pattern.

"Can we eat here? I'm getting hungry. Something in that basket smells awfully good." Rob glanced at the wicker hamper.

Angela nodded. The tangy air was whetting her appetite, too.

Rob yanked a blanket from the back end of the car with a flourish and spread it on the ground at Angela's feet.

"A throne for my princess. Just make sure you don't sit on a rock."

"Some kingdom, if this is the throne," she commented, feeling with her foot the spot on which she wanted to settle. With the basket at her feet, she began to dole out the delicacies that she had so painstakingly prepared.

"This looks wonderful! You must have gone to the deli last night and had a heyday."

"Deli!" Angela's tone sounded as if she were deeply affronted. "What an insult! I cooked this myself!"

Rob looked incredulously at the chicken leg he was holding. "And she cooks, too!" Grinning apologetically, he said, "I will never doubt you again, Angela Malone. You can do anything you set your mind to." With that Rob bit into the chicken and conversation was lost for the next few minutes.

Angela studied Rob from under hooded lids as she sat cross-legged on the blanket. He was resting his back against the little Volkswagen soaking up the heat from the sun. In faded jeans and a white sweatshirt with kangaroo pouch pocket and a hood that tumbled down his back, he looked strong but vulnerable, distant but approachable, mature but young.

*You're a man of contrasts, Rob Jordan,* Angela thought to herself. *You say I can do anything I set my mind to, but can I make you love me?*

Rob caught her staring and winked. "You're looking very serious, Angie. Anything you'd like to talk about?"

Angela felt the blushing heat bleed across her ivory skin and shook her head much too quickly.

"That good, huh?" Rob queried and dropped the question already answered by her response. "Let's go for a walk along the beach."

Angela jumped to her feet and began gathering utensils into the basket. Rob's eyes were the color of the sky overhead—and they were seeing far too much.

A cool breeze whipped Angela's hair into a black frenzy as they walked. Impulsively, she kicked away her shoes and wiggled her toes in the soft sand. Rob wandered nearer the water as she bent to retrieve the cast-off sandals. She found herself intrigued by the water-smoothed stones cast onto the beach. Rob found her moments later studying the muted red and gray, russet and black stones, idly turning them in the palm of her hand.

"Are you a rock hound?" He came up behind her silently, the wind muffling his approach.

Angela laughed. "Of sorts. I like diamonds, rubies, emeralds, those types of rocks."

"And I like these." Rob squatted down on his haunches beside her, studying first the tiny pile of stones she had amassed and then, the collector. "Simple, pretty, inexpensive. Can't beat that."

Angela sighed. Another disparity between them. But she would not allow that to mar their day. Impulsively she stood and flung her arms wide toward the water. "It's like being at the ocean, isn't it? The water is so big, so wide, you can't see land on the other side. It all reminds me how insignificant I am in the scheme of things." She turned to him, an impish twinkle in her dark eyes. "Perhaps I'm due for a humbling experience or two. Let's go hiking."

Rob took the hand she offered. This was Angela Malone at her best.

At day's end, tired but happy, Angela lay back against the tattered cushion of the Volkswagen as they sped toward Chicago. Rob watched her from the corner of his eye, his mind churning with the thoughts that so often beset him.

He had never spent a day quite like this one—charged with joy and fraught with confusion. Every moment that Angela had stood apart from him—collecting stones or feeding the gulls that landed just out of reach, begging—he had studied her. He had memorized the shape and size and look of her, embedding it on his memory forever should he come to know that she was not the woman for him. When she came near, slipping a hand around his waist or filling the pouch of his sweater with whatever she had collected, he would savor the heady scent of her perfume and the herbal aroma of her hair.

More and more he wanted her. But she still did not accept his faith. She merely tolerated it. Her questions were quick, astute; her logic, keen. But until she took that leap of faith that he knew so well, they would never have that kinship he so desired. Tormented yet hopeful, he treasured each moment, praying for more of them.

Her eyes closed, Angela didn't realize they had left the highway's main artery until Rob's little car vibrated to a halt. Her eyes flew open to meet the encompassing darkness.

"Rob, where are we?"

"A favorite spot of mine from years past."

"And just what does that mean?"

"My high-school days. It used to be the place to come and—uh—park."

"Rob Jordan! I can't believe you'd indulge in that sort of thing," Angela teased.

"Well, actually, I didn't very often. Between football, wrestling, swim team, and debate. I had a curfew nearly all year long. I didn't waste too many of my precious free nights up here. But I always thought that some day I'd like to share this place with one special girl. You know, one I didn't consider a waste of time."

Angela accepted the backhanded compliment with equanimity. "I'm flattered, Rob. Thank you." She wondered idly if he could hear her heart pounding in her chest. It was setting up such a racket in her own ears that she could hardly hear herself speak. She felt like a teenager about to receive her first kiss—excited, shy, unsure of what her body was saying, but when she dared to glance at Rob he was watching her carefully, smiling.

"Well, what are you staring at?" she challenged.

"You. You're beautiful, you know."

"Even in jeans?"

"Better in jeans. More approachable. Less intimidating."

"Intimidating, Rob? Me?"

"Very. I don't intimidate easily and you nearly scared me away."

That struck a chill in Angela. "I'm sorry, I don't mean to be."

"You're just too good at what you do. A competent woman needs a competent man. She'll frighten all the others off."

"And do you consider yourself competent, Rob?"

"Very." She could hear him shift positions and feel the warmth of his body near hers.

Then the silence of the night enveloped the car. Angela was conscious of the soft nuzzling sounds Rob's lips made against her neck, her cheek, her lips. . . . Rob's breathing deepened in the otherwise soundless vehicle.

Angela felt giddy. The world outside them disappeared. A warm glow spread through her like rivers of sunlight. She felt her own breath quicken and instinctively she pulled him toward her, hungry for more of him.

"Uumph!" Rob pulled away rubbing his chest and screwing his face into a disgusted grimace. "Now I know why the only car my parents would let me drive was a Volkswagen. The steering wheel and stick shift are as good as having a chaperone peering over the back seat!" He attempted to settle his lengthy legs in a more comfortable position away from the gear shift, but the steering mechanism thwarted him again.

Angela, covering her twitching mouth with open hands, began to shake in silent laughter. It was as if Rob were intent on twisting himself into a pretzel around the metal barriers.

"Somehow, I hadn't imagined the moment would be quite like this." His dry humor saved her, and the laughter that had been building bubbled out, spilling over both of them.

"I'll have more respect for teenagers from now on," Angela stammered, her voice cracking with laughter. "They have more obstacles to overcome than I'd remembered."

"They do if their parents are wise and make them drive economy cars," Rob rejoined before adding, "I must have filled out since high school. I'm sure things weren't this crowded then!"

"Rob, you are the sweetest, funniest, craziest man I have ever met!" Angela took his face between her palms and scrunched it into an unwilling pucker. Then she placed a wet, noisy and enthusiastic kiss on his lips. "Now," she added, "let's get out of here."

"Gotcha." Rob turned the ignition, and the lamented car jerked to life. They drove back to Angela's apartment in companionable silence, her head resting on his shoulder. As they rolled to a stop, Angela lifted her head from his shoulder and asked, "Monday?"

"How about lunch? I have plans for Monday evening."

"Okay. See you at twelve." Angela agreed, slightly jealous of whatever his evening schedule might involve. She found herself longing to be included in every minute of Rob's day, but he didn't elaborate so she slipped from the car and waved as he headed for home.

Irritated by Pete's persistent gossiping and overwhelmed by the stacks of work that had accumulated on her desk, Angela decided to slip out of the office early and surprise Rob. Perhaps he could be cajoled into taking a longer, more leisurely lunch hour.

Still piqued by Rob's plans for the evening, which didn't include her, she wanted to squeeze every moment she could out of Rob's hectic day for herself. His company had a soothing affect upon her. Even the secretaries were more friendly and less wary these days. Perhaps she *had* been more intimidating than she realized. She had mellowed under Rob's influence.

When no one answered her knock, she stepped into his office. Empty. Perhaps coming early had been a poor idea after all. Killing time, she idly meandered over to the appointment book on Rob's desk. It would tell her where he was.

"Deposition—H. Green case—9–12 A.M."

So that's where he had gone. Glancing at her watch, she wondered where his secretary was and how she would fill the remaining time. Her eyes fell back to the open schedule and traveled down the page. She saw her own name and the lunch hour blanked out next to it and smiled. But farther down, in the evening hours, was another entry in Rob's own scrawl.

*Dinner with Kim at The Willows—7:00.*

There was that name again. The one that cropped up with such unbecoming regularity.

Kim? The Willows? That was the finest in dining that Chicago had to offer! Rob couldn't afford to take anyone to The Willows! Several of her friends had been taken there the night their husbands proposed— a dark and dreamy place with fresh roses for the ladies. Why would Rob be dining in such a romantic spot? And just *who* was this Kim? Visions of lissome blondes and voluptuous redheads danced before her, reminding her of all the things she was not. Why should Rob prefer her, after all? A petite, black-haired intellectual was hardly the answer to a man's dreams!

A surge of envy and resentment billowed through her. Hurt and angry, she turned from the tell-tale page, tears welling in her dark eyes.

Jealousy had been an unfamiliar emotion to Angela. What she'd wanted she always received. Until now. And the green-eyed monster raged within her with all the fury at its disposal.

And into the office during this internal war walked Rob.

"Hi! Ready for lunch? I'd better go right now. I saw my secretary coming down the hall. I've got a big day today!" Rob slung his briefcase onto his desk, obscuring the revelatory appointment book.

By accident or by design? Angela wondered. Then the injured fury that had been building inside her spewed forth. "Big day, you say? Well, don't let me get in the way!" Rob's jaw dropped in amazement as she spoke. "But, then again, by the looks of things, you haven't let me get in the way at all!"

"What in the world are you talking about?" Rob grasped her by the shoulders, but she shook herself free and backed toward the open door, the imprints of his fingers still burning through her blouse.

"You should know better than anyone what I'm talking about, but I'll give you a hint." She spat out the words with a fury. "It's your juggling act, Rob. You did a good job keeping me in the dark, but now the fun is over. There's only *one* of us left to toy with!''

Angela turned and ran from the office leaving Rob standing aghast in the middle of the room.

He held out a hand, but when she turned toward him there was an icy resentment in her eyes. She grasped the handle of the open door and pulled it shut behind her. The finality of the sound reverberated throughout the room.

Angela spent the noon hour in a small park near her office pacing lengths as long as her legs would stretch. Unaccustomed to tears and given to action, she stamped off some of the furious energy her jealousy had stoked.

*He'll pay for this!*

Back at her office, Angela struggled for normalcy. She avoided Pete with his sharp eyes and prying tongue, however. If he began to ask questions she was not sure she could hold up. This was far too painful. Though they had made no promises, she felt Rob had been unfaithful. And now it was his turn. She would show him how it hurt. And she didn't care whom she used to make her point.

The intercom buzzed on her desk and her secretary's well modulated voice drifted into the room. "Ms. Malone. If you have a few minutes, Michael Renfrow would like to speak with you."

*Renfrow! The engineer penguin!*

"Show him in." Angela steeled herself for the encounter. She had fielded his calls since their disastrous date, fearing he would attempt to see her.

"Hello, Angela. It's nice to see you again."

"Michael, what can I do for you?"

"Ahem. Several things. First of all, I'd like you to look over these items and respond to them. Contracts and the like. If you would tell me when you might have a chance to read them, I'll make an appointment. I apologize for just dropping in today, but I was nearby and they were on the front seat of the car and—"

"Next week will be fine, Michael. Now was there anything else?" Angela pressed to get on with things.

"Well, I was wondering—"

"Yes?"

"If you wouldn't want to—"

"Want to what, Michael?"

"Have dinner with me tonight." Angela groaned mentally, wishing she'd never let him into the office. But Michael continued, "I've always wanted to dine at The Willows because I've heard that it's a very special place. I'd be honored if you'd go with me."

The Willows! The opportunity was already presenting itself! Very soon Rob could know what she had felt. Michael Renfrow would do quite nicely—acceptably attractive, well-dressed, fairly wealthy according to Jenna. Quite nicely indeed.

"Thank you, Michael. I believe I will." Angela conceded, her mind already darting ahead.

"You will?" the astonished Michael asked. It was apparent that he had not expected his question to be received with such willingness. "Great! I'll pick you up at eight."

Angela's mind raced back to the appointment book. "Can you make that seven, Michael?"

"Fine! Fine! Even better! I'll see you then." He backed out the door, but Angela had already turned her attention to his file and did not even look up as she heard the door close behind him. She would see enough of him at seven.

When Michael arrived, Angela met him at the door, eager to expedite her scheme. She had chosen a beaded white evening dress that glittered and danced in the light like a crystal chandelier. Draped over her shoulders, the dress dipped at the back to her waist, revealing a luminescent expanse of ivory skin. She wore no jewelry, the dress being its own adornment.

171

Michael's eyes widened at the vision and expanded even further as Angela tossed a white fox cape over her shoulders. She had sprayed a hint of glitter onto her sleek ebony hair. The black and white played against each other in a dramatic illusion broken only by the sparkle of her dress and her hair in the low light of the apartment.

"You'll be the most beautiful woman at The Willows. There's no doubt about that!" Michael gushed. Angela only eyed him speculatively. She hoped so. That had been her intent.

She nearly lost her nerve as they stepped from Michael's Mercedes and turned it over to a driver at the door.

Rob would hate a place like this! Why would he bring a woman here? To impress, like Michael had? To propose? An icy chill slithered along her spine, and she thought, *Anything but that! Please anything but that!*

Once inside, her eyes darted about, looking for Rob, both anxious and fearful to see the much-resented Kim. Each time a beautiful woman passed them on the way to the powder room, Angela's eyes darted toward the main dining room to see which man was waiting.

"Hello, Angela, I didn't expect to run into you here." The familiar voice sent spasms through her, but she turned nonchalantly to meet the piercing blue eyes.

"Rob, I'd like you to meet my date, Michael Renfrow." Angela grasped the engineer's elbow and pulled him to her.

"Michael, this is Rob Jordan, a business acquaintance of mine." Her escort, eyeing the handsome man, stole a possessive arm around Angela's waist in an acutely familiar gesture. He was obviously marking his territory, wanting there to be no mistake who's date this was.

Rob watched the cozy touch, and his eyes followed Michael's hand downward where it rested on Angela's hip in a suggestive display. Angela made no move to shed the offending hand though her insides rebelled at the unwelcome caress. Her eyes dared Rob to challenge them, and she saw unspoken pain cloud the blue orbs, but his gaze never wavered.

"I'd like you to meet my date, too."

Angela steeled herself for the moment. Pain clutched at her heart. A beautiful buxom blonde sailed up to them and Angela nearly fainted. There was no competing with a body such as that one.

"This is my very special date. This is Kim," Rob said with some pride.

Angela attempted to lock eyes with the blonde, but she sailed by into the arms of a man standing to Angela's right. Suddenly Angela began to look around, searching for Kim. Her eyes fell downward until they rested on a very small Korean boy with straight black hair and the largest, brownest almond-shaped eyes she had ever seen.

"Kim?" she whispered, her heart sinking.

"Hello, pretty lady." The little boy stuck out a hand to shake hers, his scrawny wrist protruding far too much out of the frayed little suit jacket.

Angela grasped the tiny warm hand.

"Kim's mother works here. In the kitchen," she heard Rob explain. "And tonight they said she could have guests—on the house! So Kim and I are here for dinner."

So that was the special evening Rob had spoken of!

"Mister Rob is my best friend. He's great! He's teaching me to play baseball and swim and even roller-skate! Mr. Rob watches me when my mother can't find a baby-sitter. I wish he could watch me all the time." The boy chattered like a squirrel, and Rob smiled down at him, touseling the shiny head affectionately.

Angela watched the exchange, heartsick. Where was her trust? Why hadn't she believed that Rob lived as he said he did—honestly, straightforward, true? Mortified by what she had thought and done, she wanted to rush away, but the suggestive hold Michael had on her hip prevented her.

Rob was speaking again. "Kim and I had planned to come at seven, but his mother called and asked us to come earlier. Because of more late reservations, I suppose. So we're on our way home to play some games. Right, Kim?"

"Right!" The boy took Rob's hand and led him toward the front porticos. Rob paused for a fleeting instant in front of Angela and whispered, "Goodbye, Angela." A dark, unreadable sadness filmed his eyes.

Chilled by the fearsome finality of his words, Angela reached toward him, but Michael gave a little jerk on her hip, edging her into the dining room.

He was gone. Perhaps forever. Driven away by her insane jealousy. She had chosen her own destiny and already she despised it.

## CHAPTER 11

ANGELA STUDIED THE JEWELER'S gem case, staring blankly at the winking stones. She plucked a dinner ring from its velvet bed and slid it on the ring finger of her left hand. It sparkled in the light, throwing colorful fires as the myriad of hues in its depths danced.

She eyed the four-digit price tag dispassionately. If she purchased it, it would be the third piece of expensive jewelry this week. But she doubted it would make her any happier than the first. Her possessions had lost their power to please, it seemed. And these bright baubles held no more capacity for fulfillment than those she already owned.

"Is there something else I might show you, madam?" The haughty clerk queried. "Something in a lesser gem, perhaps?"

"No. Thank you." Angela slipped the ring from her finger and gathered her clutch and gloves. She was finally beginning to realize what she wanted—and it wasn't a diamond dinner ring gracing her left hand. A simple gold ring would do. A plain yellow band. A wedding band from Rob. And money alone could not buy that.

Rob had withdrawn, no doubt hurt and confused by the display she had rendered that night at The Willows. She had attempted to cheer her mood by purchasing expensive baubles, but when that failed, as it had again today, she threw herself into her work, submerging the pain in complicated legal briefs and extensive research. Even Kevin had not called. His silence assured Angela that Rob had not deserted the boy along with her. But then again, Kevin had done nothing to deserve it. . . .

"Good afternoon, Mees Malone."

Angela's head snapped up, and her eyes met the wizened, leathery face of Rico Fowler. "Hello, Mr. Fowler. How nice to see you. I planned to have my secretary call you today."

"Do you know about my car, Mees Malone? I have been very worried. I do not want to go to jail. They told me if I didn't pay, I might go to jail."

Angela warmed to the little man. At least here was one area in which she could feel good. And even Fowler's presence in her life was of Rob's doing.

"I have good news. I've discovered that the car you purchased has been bought and sold by the same car dealership five times in the last eighteen months."

"My car? I don't understand!"

"It seems, Mr. Fowler, that that particular car dealership makes a habit of selling faulty cars and then repossessing them when the owners become dissatisfied and refuse to pay. Over sixty-five percent of all their transactions in the last twenty-four months have ended in repossession within three months' time. We should have no trouble convincing a judge that you were used and abused by that company. So please don't worry any more. Everything will be fine. I'll contact you when our case comes before the court. Until that time, just relax. You've done nothing wrong."

The smile on Fowler's face was like the sun breaking through the clouds. He grabbed Angela's hand and began pumping it until her shoulder ached with the exertion.

"Thank you! Thank you! Thank you! You are as wonderful as Mr. Rob! Thank you!"

Angela patted the man's hand and pulled her throbbing arm free from his grip. "You're welcome, Mr. Fowler. I've enjoyed working for you." She smiled at him as he trotted down the street waving his hat joyously back toward her. When he turned the corner, she settled again into her reverie.

Then the impact of what she had told him hit her. *I did enjoy working for him! Free of charge. Without pay. Gratis.* Out of the goodness of her heart. She had enjoyed every minute of it!

Her heart began to race with the realization flooding through her. Rob was gone, but he had left a legacy. He had shown her the joy in helping others. Angela realized wryly that she had better take advantage of her new found lesson. There was little other joy in her life right now.


"Angela, I don't know what's going on with you, but it's got to stop!"

"Start at the beginning, Pete, and make sense. Bursting into my office and yelling won't help your problem, whatever it is." Angela looked up from her desk at her red-faced associate.

"It's the string of clients you've had wandering through here. Henshaw, Radison and Grimes have *all* asked me about it! The secretaries are going wild. They've said that your billable hours have fallen way off, and it's no wonder! Not one of these new clients looks like they have a dime to their names! What's gotten into you?"

"If I want to accept new clients, I have that right. You know that, Pete."

"And what kinds of things are you doing for these people, Angela. Surely not estate planning!"

"Child-custody disputes, workman's-compensation claims, loss of entitlements—that type of thing."

"You can't charge peanuts for those things, Angela! What happened to the girl who decided which clients she would take by the cut of their clothes and the number of their jewels?"

"She's gone, Pete. And I don't miss her a bit. She wasn't as smart as she thought she was."

"She was better at making money than whoever you are now!"

"Don't be so sure!" Angela wagged a finger in front of Pete's face. "Something interesting happened in court yesterday with Mr. Fowler."

"The infamous car case? Oh, please." Pete flopped into the chair and turned his nose skyward.

"Listen to this! Not only did I get Fowler's contract set aside for fraud, the judge, convinced that the dealership had a larger scheme of abuse against the entire community, awarded attorney's fees as well! I'm getting paid a hefty sum for the Fowler case—and I didn't expect a penny!"

Pete's jaw dropped. "But that's rarely done, Angela. You couldn't know that would happen."

"It wouldn't have mattered. I would have tried the case anyway. The money is just a bonus."

"Just a bonus. The very last words I ever expected to hear from the lips of Angela Malone. Incredible." Pete jumped to his feet and trotted from the office.

Angela nodded. It was incredible. And she had been remembering something Rob had told her long ago about representing Fowler. "I know it's difficult, but trust that it will work out. In the long run you'll gain more by giving of yourself."

He was right, of course. Rob usually was. And wise. He knew which things in life were important. If only she had learned sooner he might not be gone!

Tears welled in her eyes and began spilling down her cheeks, but she wiped them quickly away as Pete shot back into the room, excitement sparkling in his eyes and energy crackling from every pore.

"You'll never guess what I just heard in the hallway!"

"I probably won't, Pete. I'm not usually interested in information gleaned in the halls." Angela turned back to her books, hiding red eyes.

"The Simmons suit has been settled out of court."

Angela's head shot up. Rob had done it!

"What are the terms, Pete. Did you hear?"

"Caught your interest after all, didn't I? Well, as far as I can tell, it's a fair and equitable solution for all. That's a miracle in itself. This Rob Jordan worked out an arrangement so that Simmons is committed to build government subsidized low-income housing units in equal number to the ones he tears out. They are to be built concurrently with Simmons's other structures. So Hannah Green and all her cohorts will have a place to live, after all!"

Breathlessly Angela asked, "And what does Simmons have to say about all of this?"

"Believe it or not, he agreed amicably. He saw that he could be tied up for years otherwise. He's not even mad. There seems to be a grudging admiration for his victorious opponent. Jordan proposed the idea of a government-grant package to guarantee a long-term return on Simmons's capital. The government will subsidize the difference between what Hannah Green and the rest pay for rent and what Simmons needs to get a return on his investment. Actually, from what I can gather, everyone in the office seems to think Jordan is a genius. I'll bet he gets a job offer from this firm within the year!" Pete whistled under his breath. "What a coup!"

Angela leaned back in her chair, drained. Rob had salvaged her job as well. Simmons and her employers would no longer need a scapegoat. Her position was secure. But Rob had accomplished even more. She had learned some profound lessons about herself and about the God Rob espoused.

Once Pete told his story he dashed back into the hall, hoping for details. Angela opened her desk drawer and reached for the purchase she had hidden there.

It was a Bible. A brand new Bible. The pages stuck together slightly as she leafed through them looking for that special passage. Matthew. She knew it was in here; she'd seen it before. Finally she found it and turned to chapter five and read: "Let your light so shine before men, that they may see your good works and give glory to your Father who is in heaven."

For the first time, Angela saw in this passage potential for her own life. Perhaps she, too, could serve, could shine. She devoured the pages, seeking the messages Rob found so entrancing and became more hungry for its sagacity with each progressing page. An aching loneliness beset her each time a favorite verse of Rob's came to light but she hung over the pages, wrapped in their wisdom, eager to fill the void she felt in her heart.

Finally her eyes were too scratchy and her back too sore to continue to lean over the desk, savoring the pages. Her physical hunger gnawed at her insides like the spiritual hunger she was finally satiating. Sadly she wished that she could call Rob and ask him to join her for dinner, but chagrin and regret hindered her. Facing Rob after her brazen display seemed too humiliating. She could only hope that he would forgive her for her lack of trust in him and her tawdry play at revenge.

Idly she wondered if Emily Jordan had changed the furniture in Rob's apartment again. Emily had called recently, seemingly unaware of the rift between Angela and her son, to say that she and Carl were taking an extended vacation soon. She had wanted Angela to know that she was welcome at their home even though they would be gone. She was as thoughtful as her son.

Slipping a granola bar from the bottom drawer of her desk, Angela sauntered into the hall and ventured toward the coffee room. Supper alone seemed so unappealing that she decided to make do with the bar and a can of juice from the vending machine.

The normally noisy room was silent but for the persistent drone of the appliances. Dropping quarters into the slot, Angela punched a lighted button and with a rattle and a thump a can of orange juice landed in the slot.

Disengaging her juice from the dispenser, she headed toward a table littered with paper cups and the day's newspaper. Lethargically chewing on the crunchy oatmeal bar, Angela flipped through the pages of the paper, scanning for news that might interest her.

Suddenly, a news story caught her eye and she began to read, the meager meal forgotten:

**"BOY IN SERIOUS CONDITION AFTER BEING BUMPED BY HIT-AND-RUN DRIVER**—Kim Wang, aged eight, of 414 Fairdayle, is listed in serious condition after being hit by an unidentified driver near his grade school. The boy is suffering from head injuries as well as several broken bones. The police are looking for a blue, 1984 model . . ."

Angela's eyes drifted off the page. Kim was injured. She knew with a certainty where Rob would be. And perhaps he needed her. If not needing her especially, he would still need *someone* to comfort him. Tenderhearted Rob would hate to go through this alone.

Leaving the juice can unopened, Angela ripped off the portion of paper containing Kim's story and raced from the room. Fortunately, the hospital was listed. Still clutching the shred of paper, Angela gathered her purse and sweater from her office and ran, dodging outgoing traffic, to her car. If Kim was as badly injured as the paper said, every minute might count.

Frustrated nearly to tears by rush-hour traffic, it took Angela an hour to reach her destination. Her hands were trembling by the time she pulled into the visitor parking lot and pulled the little paper tongue from the time ticket machine spewing them out.

She glanced at the card she had just pulled from the humped metal machine. Six fifty five. If there were any reason to be at the hospital, Rob would be there. He would only leave if . . . Angela petitioned silently, *Please, not that!*

Antiseptic vapors assaulted her nostrils as she opened the thick glass doors leading into the waiting room of the vast medical facility. The tile beneath her feet gleamed like polished glass, and she wondered wildly if anyone ever had the desire to skate down the endless hallways in stocking-footed abandon.

"You're losing it entirely, Malone," she muttered to herself. The tension was making her giddy. That, and the thought that she would be seeing Rob again for the first time in weeks.

Her heart, thrumming madly in her chest, seemed to pulse and swell until it inhabited the entire cavity. Gulping for air, she immediately regretted inhaling more of the noisome infirmary fumes.

*Kim. Rob.* Angela gathered an invisible cloak of composure about her and strode purposefully toward the information desk.

"I'm here to visit the little boy who was injured by the hit-and-run driver. Could you tell me which room he is in?"

"He's on the third floor. Room 345. But you'll have to check with the head nurse up there. I don't know whether or not visitors are allowed."

"Thank you." Angela turned toward the wall of elevators flanking the right side of the visitors' area and stepped briskly to catch one whose yawning jaws were just closing on the lobby level.

She faced directly forward, never glancing to the right or left, her mind reeling with the possibilities that might face her. Kim's well-being. She remembered his bright eyes and the gentlemanly thrust of his hand as he greeted her that fateful night at The Willows with his "Hi, pretty lady!" Dark thoughts clouded her mind as she thought of the child flung against a fast moving vehicle . . . head injuries . . . most frightening of all.

And Rob. What would he say when he saw her? They hadn't spoken since that awful night. She could still feel Michael Renfrow's possessive hand on her hip and see the hurt and bewilderment in Rob's eyes. Surely not even Rob's charitable nature could tolerate such abuses! Perhaps he would not speak to her, but she had to try.

Fearful of rebuff, she was still more afraid of spending the rest of her life without him. And she would soon know what her fate would be.

She could see Rob from the far end of the hall. He was slumped forward in a chair, his face buried in his hands, his elbows resting on jean-clad thighs. His hair was spiky and unkempt as though he had been running his fingers through the tendrils in frustration or dismay. His shoulders hunched under the coffee-brown corduroy suit jacket he wore. A brown and blue plaid shirt collar peeked out from under the uptilted collar of the jacket.

"Rob." Angela spoke softly, not wanting to startle him, but he jumped up like a shot, nearly upturning the half-filled styrofoam coffee cup at his feet. She felt herself draw in a sharp breath as his eyes devoured her. They were the same bright blue as the sweater he wore under his jacket and their startling intensity nearly took her breath away. She wondered briefly how she could have forgotten his eyes. It was like forgetting the color of the sky on a summer day.

He took a step forward—then hesitated. His hands hung at his sides slowly clenching and unclenching, the thumb of his right hand rubbing imperceptibly over the first knuckle of his index finger—the only movement belying any agitation.

Faltering at first, Angela edged forward, but an aid, pushing a cart loaded with juice and glasses passed in front of her. For a moment her goal was obscured. Wavering, Angela had turned to flee when she heard the soft, familiar voice.

"Wait."

Casting her fears and inhibitions to the wind, she turned back, half running, half walking toward him, tears blinding her pathway. She came upon him hard and fast, running directly into the open arms that waited and she buried her nose in the cottony softness of his sweater, inhaling the heady fragrance of him.

She had dampened his entire front before she raised her head from his chest, reluctant to leave the strong, warm thumping of his heart.

He was more beautiful than she had remembered him. Bigger. Broader. Incredibly wonderful.

"I'm glad you came."

His words brought her back to the troubles at hand. Her own personal torment was of no consequence at this moment. It could wait until she knew if the child was safe.

"Kim. How is he?"

"Bad, Angela. He hasn't come out of the coma yet. His mother is with him right now." Angela felt the trembling in Rob's limbs and she pushed him gently toward the chair. When the back of his calves met the molded plastic rim, they collapsed, seemingly of their own accord, and he was down. His head dropped into his hands again, and while running agitated fingers through the sandy mop, he began to speak.

"He was coming to see me, Angela. For the first time alone. His mother had to be at work early, and I said I'd watch him. I told her I was too busy to pick him up. She said she'd leave him at the street corner and he could walk to my office. His big adventure! Why didn't I take the time to pick him up?" Rob looked at her in anguish. He drew his hands across his face, his fingertips following the line of his brows, thumbs resting on his jaw and reiterated the complaint. "I should have picked him up."

"You can't blame yourself for this, Rob! It was an accident! Since when does placing blame solve anything?"

"You don't understand. . . ."

"But I *do!* I've been blaming myself for a lot of things lately—and it's blame I've justly earned. But it's not helping, Rob. I've decided that the only thing that will help is starting where you are—right now and at this moment and doing what you can to pick up the pieces. Go forward. Not back."

"So what do you recommend I do for that poor little guy?" Rob's muffled question held a hint of sarcasm.

"You can pray for him, Rob."

Rob raised his head in amazement, and stared at Angela. "Am I hearing that from you?"

"I've come a long way in the past few weeks, Rob. And I've finally discovered what you've known all along. That we have to trust our lives—and Kim's—to God."

The first hint of a smile played on Rob's features. "Pray? Here? In the hall? Where people can see me? And risk having you throw a coat over my head so people won't stare?"

"Anywhere you please. It won't embarrass me any longer."

A pleased light flickered in Rob's eyes as the import of what she was saying began to dawn on him. "Angela, do you mean . . ."

All she could do was nod, for at that moment,

185

Kim's mother stepped from his room looking for Rob. A flicker of fear darted across his face before he noticed the broad smile on Mrs. Wang's countenance.

"He's awake! He wants to see you, Mr. Jordan! My little boy is awake!"

Rob gathered the older woman in a bone-crushing bear hug and planted a noisy, relieved kiss on her cheek before discarding her in the chair he had just evacuated and bolting into the room. A second later his head reappeared around the corner of the door, and he beckoned for Angela.

Hesitantly, she stepped into the blue and white room where her eyes fell on the tiny figure resting in a large and sterile bed. Kim's hair, as black as her own, feathered across the pristine white pillow. His face, nearly as pale as the pillow beneath him, would have been lost but for the wonderful almond eyes that winked and blinked in pleasure as Rob entered.

Then those eyes, the color of semi-sweet chocolate and tins of shoe polish, fell on Angela. They widened slightly and a small voice from the bed greeted her.

"Hello, pretty lady!"

Rob released the breath he had been holding, and it sighed in unison with another in the room whom they had not noticed.

"So he recognizes you two. Another good sign." A white-frocked doctor stepped from behind the dividing screen that had partially hidden him from view. It was apparent that he knew Rob as he spoke. "You can stay *two minutes*. This little guy has had more than his share today."

Angela nodded crisply as the man slipped into the hall behind them. It was as she put out her hand for Rob and reached for the warmth of his ribs beneath his coat that she felt him shudder with relief. Turning to him, she was amazed to find tears resting on his cheeks.

He grinned at her and wiped them away with the

heel of his hand as he moved toward the boy's bed—softly, almost on tip-toe, fearful of jarring the child in any way.

*The man was crying!*

Rob Jordan was springing something new upon her at every turn. Once, in the not-too-distant past, Angela would have scoffed at a man who wept. How wrong she had been! But now she knew the strength it took to show real, loving emotion. Only *true* men could weep! All the others, too insecure to let those tender emotions show, could only suffer in dry-eyed silence.

"I said two minutes!" The doctor was at the door again. Rob touched Kim's forehead with a finger so light it seemed only to graze the air above him. "Keep fighting, Tiger." Rob whispered and turned to leave, drawing Angela along with him.

In the hall, Rob gripped her elbows in a powerful lock and forced her to face him.

"We have to talk."

She nodded dumbly in response, still too buffeted by her emotions to speak.

"The Willows?"

Angela's eyes shot to his in horror only to find a gentle smile there. How could he tease at a time like this? Quickly, he went on.

"Okay, then. How about my place?"

Relief flooded through her. She *would* get to see that ramshackle and wonderful place. Even if he could not—would not—understand what she had done, at least there could be a proper goodbye.

With that thought, terror closed around her like a shroud.

## CHAPTER 12

ROB FREED THE LOCK on his apartment door and kicked it open in front of Angela. Taking a deep breath, she stepped inside. Her eyes had fluttered closed in anticipation of what miracles Emily Jordan had wrought in the dumpy room this time.

Her eyes opened . . . and opened . . . and opened as the most frilled and ruffled display of early American furniture ever made met her eyes.

"This is the worst yet. Mother's gone too far this time. And I told her so."

Angela began to giggle as her eyes followed the tucked and tufted print fabric stretched across the couch to the point where generous ruffles swept the floor in dainty splendor.

There were eagles everywhere. They were waving with open wings from a black milk can transformed into an ashtray. They soared in antiqued gold from the bases of lamps. They were cross-stitched into pillows, trimmed with eyelet, and scattered about the room. It was a veritable eagle paradise. Both side chairs, rockers, were replete with spindles and more tiny print fabric in beige, red, and navy. Angela had to quell the urge to salute.

"This is quite . . . amazing. Somehow I would never have guessed it of your mother."

"She prides herself on being open-minded, Angela. You know, something for everyone's style. But this isn't the worst of it."

"You mean there's more?" Angela swallowed hard. This room, to her sophisticated leanings, was the ultimate in bad taste. What could be worse?

"She said I could eat on it, Angela. And you know what *that means!* What am I going to do?"

Laughter bubbled up as she studied the horrified expression on Rob's face. The very thought of having to keep these monstrosities made him nauseous. She could read it in the seasick way he kept glancing at the couch.

"I've been having trouble sleeping, knowing this is out here. It's like a B-movie, 'The Eagle That Ate Chicago.' And I think mother believes that she's discovered my true personality. I've never been so insulted in my life!"

"Never, Rob?" The words came softly, fearfully. Their laughter subsided and he stared at her. Quietly. Unmoving.

She wished that he would say or do something. Anything. His silent gaze was more painful than a thrashing.

Finally he spoke, and perversely she then wished he hadn't for it made the guilt and longing pool in her throat until she thought she might choke. "You're right, Angela. You provided the ultimate insult."

"And I've come to apologize." He turned away slightly, allowing his shoulder to face her, his expression hidden. "Don't turn away, Rob. Let me explain."

His breath gushed out in a half sigh, half sob. "Okay. Explain away."

Angela drew a deep breath. That's exactly what she had to do—explain away the hurt and the mistrust and the inevitable resentment she had engendered. She wished desperately for a court room and a judge where she knew her arguments would be heard dispassionately. Here, her judge was also the injured party, and she had no inkling of how deep his wounds festered.

"I went to The Willows that night because I knew you would be there, Rob. I finagled Michael into taking me there. I went there planning to—teach you a lesson. And it seems I was the one who got the education! Who said 'A little knowledge is a dangerous thing?' How right they were!" Angela laughed humorlessly, a dry empty laugh.

"I don't understand, Angela. What was I supposed to be learning? And what did I do to deserve it?" The hurt was floating nearer the surface in Rob's voice now. He sounded as if he were nearly drowning in it.

"I went to your office at noon that day. Do you remember?"

"Do I? You bit my head off and spit it out on the carpet! I spent the rest of the day wondering what I'd done wrong."

"Wrong? You left your appointment book open. And it fell into misguided hands—mine."

"But I don't understand!" Rob nearly wailed, his frustration and confusion mounting.

"Kim. I saw that you were having dinner at The Willows with Kim!"

"So?" Rob shrugged.

"*So*," Angela spoke each word with precision, "I thought that Kim was another woman!"

Confusion, doubt, anger, and finally understanding played across Rob's features, like shadows dancing. Then his countenance cleared and his private puzzle was solved. "You were *jealous?*"

"Insanely. Frantically. Unparalleled in this century." Angela nodded ruefully.

The tension that she had been reading in his shoulders slid away, and he smiled his first genuine, unguarded smile. "You set that up to make me jealous?"

"Grade school stuff, I know. When you introduced us to Kim, and here was this little tiny doll of a child, I nearly died. And by that time the wretched Michael thought he had me permanently in his clutches. I swear, his hand was pasted to my hip with Super Glue! I made him take me home immediately. I couldn't stay and pretend to enjoy myself after what I'd done."

"You should have, you know." Rob studied her as he spoke.

A ball of tension plummeted in her belly. He hadn't forgiven her after all. She ventured a meek, "Why?"

"Because I'll never be able to take you there. You missed your last chance."

"My last chance?" she inquired weakly, her watery legs threatening to buckle.

"Well, I'm certainly not going to allow Michael Renfrow or any one else to do my job for me!"

"Your job?"

"As your escort! You'll just have to come to grips with the fact that you'll probably never eat at The Willows again. Unless you pay for it, of course."

Relieved tears coursed down Angela's cheeks as she fell into the open arms Rob offered. His cheek found hers, and as he wiped away the salty droplets, she could feel the first sproutings of the rough stubble of his beard.

He set her back from him a bit and studied the now chafed and tear stained face. "I should be flattered, you know."

"How can you say that?" Angela snuffled, feeling less and less attractive with each passing moment and caring little.

"That you'd go to such lengths to make me sit up

and take notice. Apparently I wasn't doing my job before—making you feel secure. I'll do better from now on."

It was then that Angela really set up a sobbing wail, scaring Rob in the process. *He was apologizing!* He had turned this into a predicament of his own making, freeing her from blame. He had more than met her half way. He had made the trip alone, and Angela was profoundly touched.

Her emotional outburst was subsiding under Rob's tender hand, smoothing her silken charcoal head and whispering untranslatable words into her ear, when the doorbell rang.

"Rats!" Rob muttered.

Angela, enough recovered from her emotional storm, asked innocently, "Do they grow big enough to reach the doorbell in this neighborhood?" For that she found herself pushed back onto the couch as Rob jumped up to answer.

The smile she had engendered only grew at the sight of his visitor.

"Kevin! Hi, buddy! Haven't seen you for a while."

"Hi. I'm supposed to give you a message—oh, hi, Ms. Malone. Gee, I'm glad you're here! I was going to your office next."

"So what's the big message?" Rob asked, his eyes still on Angela's flushed face.

"My dad wants to see both of you in his office. As soon as possible."

"What?" Rob and Angela yelped together. Had Simmons found out about their befriending Kevin?

"For what, Kevin? Do you know?"

"Yeah. But my dad told me to stay out of it. That it was his business. I'm just supposed to find you both and bring you there. Can you come right now?"

Rob shot Angela a worried look. If Simmons sent the boy after them, he knew the truth. Only Kevin's relaxed demeanor seemed out of place for the trouble that might be brewing.

Angela flipped open a compact and tried to mend the ravages of her tears and Rob's infant beard. She slicked a comb through her shiny tresses and stood to meet the two waiting men. Whatever Simmons had in store she could handle now that she knew Rob had forgiven her.

The Simmons complex was as Angela had remembered it—a compilation of bold geometric shapes constructed into office buildings and attached by skyways. People walked above their heads in futuristic bubblelike tubes, oblivious to pedestrians below.

"He is a genius, you know," Rob whispered into Angela's ear as they admired the multi-tiered fountain that cascaded water from a plumbed Simmons' logo at its peak.

Angela nodded dumbly. To acquire this much in one short lifetime took genius—and blazing good fortune. But Simmons was a good steward of his possessions. The patches of ground that weren't paved were filled with carpets of highly fertilized and manicured grass or riotous flower displays. A maintenance man with a canvas bag slung over one shoulder spent his time spearing every wisp of litter almost before it had a chance to hit the ground.

A flower wagon and a vendor's food truck were parked on the outskirts of the central courtyard. Even they were emblazoned with the Simmons logo.

"He likes to keep everything within his control, I see." Rob commented casually as Kevin fell behind to speak with a friend.

"He even owns the hot-dog vendor! What's he going to do to a pair of meddlers?" Angela hissed.

"We've done nothing wrong, Angela. Befriending his son is hardly criminal."

"Let's just hope *he* sees it that way!"

Kevin joined them again and the threesome fell silent.

"My dad's office is this way." Kevin led them through a maze of security guards with a wave of his hand.

"Looks like you've been spending a little time here, Kevin," Rob commented.

"Some. That's why I haven't been around too much in the past couple of weeks." Before Kevin could go on, they came to an elevator marked "Private." It opened with barely a whisper, and the three stepped in. There was a single disk to push—an unmarked button.

As they whizzed skyward, Rob commented. "This is pretty classy for my blood. I'd better not stay too long. I get used to things rather easily."

Angela was thinking the same thing. Rob, standing beside her, was massaging a tender spot in the small of her back, relaxing and exciting her at the same moment. She had very easily become accustomed to his touch. In fact, the thought of all others repelled her. But she edged away from the idle motion. She had no guarantees about Rob Jordan. If she let her guard down now, it would be far more painful if he left her later.

Rob noticed the evasive motion and raised one eyebrow in a quirky question. But before he could pursue Angela's skittish behavior, the elevator door swooshed open on a plush green jungle on the penthouse level.

"Come on, Dad's office is this way." Kevin skirted a trickling fountain and a myriad of green foliage under a skylight canopy. Angela could hear birds twittering from somewhere in the center, and a bold red and green parrot startled her with a loud screech just over her right shoulder.

"That thing scared me!" she gasped, already on tenterhooks.

Kevin grinned. "That's Hiram the Horrible. He's got great feathers but a crummy disposition. He gets

194

less cocky when he's molting, but he's basically rotten. He bites, too. Mean old bird. I guess beauty isn't everything.''

Angela shot a look at Rob and read her own thoughts in his eyes. *Milton Simmons*. Was Hiram the bird world's equivalent? Angela felt the last vestiges of her confidence fading quickly. She spent the last few steps to Simmons's office mentally flagellating herself for becoming an attorney at all. Her last thoughts as they stood before Simmons's door steeled her for the encounter, *But then, how much longer will I be an attorney if Simmons has his way?*

Kevin knocked twice on the door and stepped inside. Fleetingly Angela wondered at his comfort here in this imposing complex. The boy had come a long way.

The heavy-set man was nearly obscured by a massive desk. He sat behind its vast expanse of fine leather blotter with gold tooling. He stood as they entered, and Angela wondered if it wouldn't be better to be blindfolded for one's own execution. Rob's light grasp on her elbow had tightened to viselike proportions. Her eyes fluttered shut for a moment in nervous anticipation, but when they opened they fell on the first genial look she had ever seen on Simmons's face.

"There you are! I was beginning to worry that they'd refused to come, Kevin.''

Rob screwed up his face in a puzzled frown and glanced down at Angela whose returning gaze mirrored the perplexity. It was as though they had fallen through Alice-in-Wonderland's looking glass and nothing was as expected.

Simmons grinned as best he could through thick and shiny pink jowls unused to the exercise. He lurched around his desk, a hand outstretched.

Gentlemanly Rob, unsure what Simmons had planned for the hand—a greeting or a blow—still offered his own palm to the man. Simmons clasped the extremity and pumped it furiously as astounding words flowed from his mouth.

"I've been anxious to meet you, young man! You've led me on a merry chase these past weeks. A good competitor, by jove! I've been furious with you! What fun!"

Rob's jaw slackened in dumfounded amazement. His blue eyes studied the jowly, mottled face in confusion.

"Fun?" he finally managed. "You think this has been fun?"

"Didn't you? Get with it, my boy! Anyone as bright as you should be enjoying the race, relishing the battle. I always do. How else could I have amassed this fortune of mine? Sure I've stepped on people on the way to the top, but when I find one who won't allow it—then the fun begins! And you wouldn't allow it. You've got all the things I admire in an opponent—moxie, savvy, brains. You gave me a good fight and I lost. Doesn't happen very often, you know."

Rob's shoulders had dropped two inches inside his suit coat. He had stretched his head forward in disbelief, and his hands hung lax at his sides. Angela fought the urge to close his slack mouth. He was the picture of stupefaction. Angela feared that soon he would begin to totter and fall over with that astonished expression never leaving his face.

Finally, after what seemed eons of silence, he found his voice. "You mean you *enjoy* this sort of thing? Putting old ladies out of their homes? Tormenting faceless, unpaid attorneys with truckfuls of pointless work? Disenfranchising—"

"See?" Simmons turned to Angela, his cheerfulness unsubdued. "That's why he's so good at what he does. He's won and he's still fighting! I like that in a man." Simmons paused, fumbled around a bit in his coat pocket and then added, "And a woman, too, of course."

"But I don't understand! You were furious! What's the deal, Simmons?" Rob had found his tongue and his rage.

"You're the first adversary I've ever had who managed to solve things equitably for *both* sides! By George, I think you may have found me a way to make Hannah Green's new home cash flow nicely! Wheee!" Simmons slapped a beefy thigh. "If I'd known that to begin with, none of this would have happened." Simmons cast a warning eye in Angela's direction. "That snooty firm of yours could learn a few things from this young man. If they'd take their noses out of the air and smell the flowers with him, we'd all be a lot better off!"

Angela swallowed the bubble of laughter that was beginning to build in her throat. She vowed to choke on it before she would allow it to erupt.

"Do you mind if I sit down?" Rob ventured. He looked as though his only other option were falling over.

"Please do! Kevin, where are your manners? Bring some chairs, son." As the boy scurried to do his father's bidding, Angela could see a slight smile playing at the corners of his lips. He was less surprised by this than she and Rob.

"Mr. Simmons, you'll have to explain all this to me, I'm afraid. I came here fully expecting your wrath. Instead, I'm met with smiles and congratulations."

"I told you why. I like a competent opponent. And I respect what you've done. You're fair. You're honest. You're generous. I expected you to go to bat for Hannah Green. I *didn't* expect that you'd also set out the plan to show me how to make money on her housing project. That subsidized low-income-housing package is going to work like a charm. I'm thinking of throwing in a community recreation room just for the fun of it."

197

Angela's eyes flew to Rob's face.

He glanced at her and cheerfully shrugged, the collar of his jacket tickling the golden tips of his hair. Milton Simmons seemed bent on having "fun" with the project and suddenly Rob was, too.

Watching the exchange, Simmons's eyes narrowed. Then he glanced at the boy hovering in the outer edges of the room.

"Come 'ere, kid." Kevin edged toward his father hesitantly at first, then more boldly, until he stood at the man's side. To everyone's amazement, Simmons wrapped an arm around the boy's slender waist.

"And I hear that the two of you have been doing some things for me on the sly."

Guilty glances sailed between Rob and Angela.

"That's the part I'm most grateful for. He's been a new boy these past weeks. It took me a long time to notice. I've used him as a verbal punching bag on more than one occasion, I'll admit. I didn't even consider what it might be doing to him. I'm smart in lots of ways, but a fool in others. He's told me about the time you spent with him—in spite of the Green case."

Rob's hand found Angela's beneath the line of the desk. His long warm fingers wrapped around hers in a tender clutch. Zingers of heat bolted up her arm.

Lazily, Rob inquired, "So what are you going to do about it, Simmons?"

Simmons gave another unexpected whoop of delight and hammered his fists on the desk. "You never give up, do you? I like that in a man! You've got me crawling, and you still want more! Okay, Jordan, you've got it. It's like this. Because of you two, I feel like I have a new boy on my hands. You've given us a second chance. A new son deserves a new father. And I'm going to try."

"That's the smartest thing you've said so far." Rob leaned across the wide expanse of desk to shake Milt Simmons's hand. Kevin's grin echoed his father's.

Angela's heart surged in her chest and she fought back an errant tear. She battled with the tear-wrenching tenderness that knowing Rob Jordan entailed. Her life had been easier before Rob, but she never wanted to return to that glossy, emotionless vacuum. Fortunately, Rob's quiet testimony and the studying she had done of that brand-new Bible had demonstrated a way to prevent that.

"I'd like you both to be at the ribbon-cutting ceremony for the low-income housing units. Stop at the front desk and get the time and date. Now, then, if you will excuse us, Kevin and I have a date for basketball. I may be a bit rotund, but I'm light on my feet!" Simmons patted his middle, making the watch chain looped through a buttonhole of his vest dance at his waist.

Summarily dismissed, Rob and Angela stumbled out of the room together. Simmons and son were already lost in a conversation of their own and didn't even glance up at the whispered shush of the door.

In the hall, Rob and Angela looked at each other and, in unison, collapsed against the corridor wall unable to decide whether to laugh or cry.

"Do you believe what we just heard?"

"No!" they chimed together.

"Truth is stranger than fiction, you know," Rob commented as he punched the elevator button for the trip down.

"But this is the crowning touch. And a ribbon-cutting ceremony! What do you think Simmons has up his sleeve for that?"

"Who knows. But as long as that look of bliss stays on Kevin's face I don't care. Hannah gets a home. Kevin gets a father. What else could you want?" Rob exulted.

*You!* Angela's brain screamed, but all that slipped from her lips was a wooden, "Nothing. Everything is perfect."

The weather for the ribbon-cutting ceremony was exquisite. It was as if Simmons had ordered that, too. A cloudless blue sky canopied the complex of buildings in all stages of construction. Rob and Angela had toured them, waiting for the formalities to begin.

"I'm amazed at how quickly these structures went up!" Angela commented, stepping daintily from wooden plank to wooden plank across an unexcavated area.

"Simmons's crews were ready to roll and some portions were underway before the restraining order. All that's complete so far are the housing units. But that's what really counts. People can begin to make a community here again. I'm hoping that a good share of the former residents were able to find temporary housing and can return to their new homes in the old neighborhood."

"And what about Hannah Green?"

A frown flickered across Rob's features. "I've been worrying about Hannah. I haven't been able to make contact with her for some time. I've thought of calling hospitals next. She really needs someone to look after her."

"It looks like you needn't worry any more," Angela commented.

Rob followed her gaze. Some yards away the ribbon-cutting ceremony was beginning. A monstrous red ribbon was stretched across the entry door to the housing complex. Milton Simmons, in a crisp navy suit, was wheeling Hannah Green toward that door. In Hannah's gnarled hands was a massive pair of scissors, made especially for such auspicious occasions. Her feathery white hair was tamed and curled and a corsage of red and white carnations and tea roses covered a ten-inch expanse from shoulder to breastbone.

"Well, will you look at that!" Rob came to a grinding halt as Simmons began to speak.

Simmon's voice drifted their way as he introduced Hannah as the first tenant to be moving into the complex. When the brief formalities were completed, Hannah's frail hands, quivering like leaves in the wind, lifted the massive scissors and clipped the big red ribbon.

Rob stood cheering and clapping with the rest of the crowd as Angela studied his profile. His eyes danced with delight, gleaming with that wonderful inner light he possessed.

"Whatcha thinking about, Ms. Malone?"

His question caught her off guard, and she stammered the answer. "I was just thinking about that passage in Matthew that you like so well. You, know. The light and the bushel basket. Your witness. Your light. When it shines on people—it affects them in so many ways."

"It's not *my* light, Angela, but God's. I just provide the fixture."

"I know. And I think I *finally* understand." Rob hugged her then, with a warm, supportive hug. Wordlessly they knew that they now shared a special bonding, a unifying peace. They found a rugged bench leaning against one of the half-finished buildings and sat together quietly.

Unspeaking, they rested there for several minutes until most of the crowd had dispersed. Rob rubbed his thumb along Angela's cheekbone contemplatively. She struggled to read the thoughts in his eyes, but they were dancing perversely with some private merriment.

"What's so funny?" she challenged belligerently, irritated that he didn't share his private joke. "I'm not sure I like the way your eyes are twinkling."

"There you go again. Do you realize how often you talk about light when you refer to me? I sound like a Christmas tree—twinkling and blinking and. . . ."

"You're evading the issue, Rob. What thought was causing that particular glimmer?"

He squirmed on the bench like a school boy. Then running a finger underneath his collar to loosen it, he stammered, "Ah, well, nothing really."

"Rob Jordan! 'Fess up! What were you thinking about?"

A teasing expression lit his face. "Actually, I was thinking that pretty soon you'd get a chance to see if I glowed in the *dark!*"

"Rob. . . ."

"On our honeymoon, of course!" Rob broke into a grin that sent Angela's heart racing from her throat to the pit of her stomach and back again. *Their honeymoon?*

Aloud, she captured a vestige of her former sophisticated hauteur. "You mean you're ready to take on a partner in that poverty-stricken law practice of yours?"

"Of course. The sooner the better!" Rob bit his bottom lip in that endearing way he had.

Blissfully, she lunged headlong into his arms, to accept the job offer of a lifetime. Her words were slurred, but she mumbled as Rob captured her lips with his own, "I thought you'd never ask!"

*Marriage? Indeed!*

## ABOUT THE AUTHOR

JUDY BAER, an honor graduate of Concordia College, is a wife, homemaker, and mother of two young daughters. On her birthday, her husband surprised her with a word processor, agreeing to renew the lease each year she completed a book! TENDER ADVERSARY is her second for Serenade Serenata, with another, SHADOWS ALONG THE ICE, scheduled for December. Her first inspirational romance, LOVE'S PERFECT IMAGE, received rave reviews from delighted readers across the country upon its publication in July, 1984. We are pleased to present other fine novels from this talented and committed author.

Judy writes not only for the joy of writing, but to convey her belief that Christians are granted the greatest freedom to fulfill their potential and to find joy in each other and in Him.

# *A Letter To Our Readers*

Dear Reader:

Pioneering is an exhilarating experience, filled with opportunities for exploring new frontiers. The Zondervan Corporation is proud to be the first major publisher to launch a series of inspirational romances designed to inspire and uplift as well as to provide wholesome entertainment. In order that we might better contribute to your reading enjoyment, we would appreciate your taking a few minutes to respond to the following questions and return to:

> Anne Severance, Editor
> The Zondervan Publishing House
> 1415 Lake Drive, S.E.
> Grand Rapids, Michigan 49506

1. Did you enjoy reading TENDER ADVERSARY?
   - ☐ Very much. I would like to see more books by this author!
   - ☐ Moderately
   - ☐ I would have enjoyed it more if _____

2. Where did you purchase this book? _____

3. What influenced your decision to purchase this book?
   - ☐ Cover
   - ☐ Title
   - ☐ Publicity
   - ☐ Back cover copy
   - ☐ Friends
   - ☐ Other _____

4. Please rate the following elements from 1 (poor) to 10 (superior).

☐ Heroine        ☐ Plot
☐ Hero           ☐ Inspirational theme
☐ Setting        ☐ Secondary characters

5. Which settings would you like to see in future Serenade Serenata Books?

_____  _____

_____  _____

6. What are some inspirational themes you would like to see treated in future books?

_____  _____

_____  _____

7. Would you be interested in reading other Serenade Serenata or Serenade Saga Books?

☐ Very interested
☐ Moderately interested
☐ Not interested

8. Please indicate your age range:

☐ Under 18     ☐ 25–34     ☐ 46–55
☐ 18–24       ☐ 35–45     ☐ Over 55

9. Would you be interested in a Serenade book club? If so, please give us your name and address:

Name _____

Occupation _____

Address _____

City _____ State _____ Zip _____

*Serenade Serenata Books* are inspirational romances in contemporary settings, designed to bring you a joyful, heart-lifting reading experience.

Serenade Serenata books available in your local bookstore:

Watch for other books in the *Serenade Serenata* (contemporary) series coming soon:

*Serenade Saga Books* are inspirational romances in historical settings, designed to bring you a joyful, heart-lifting reading experience.

Serenade Saga books available in your local bookstore:

#1  SUMMER SNOW, Sandy Dengler
#2  CALL HER BLESSED, Jeanette Gilge
#3  INA, Karen Baker Kletzing
#4  JULIANA OF CLOVER HILL,
    Brenda Knight Graham
#5  SONG OF THE NEREIDS, Sandy Dengler
#6  ANNA'S ROCKING CHAIR,
    Elaine Watson
#7  IN LOVE'S OWN TIME,
    Susan C. Feldhake
#8  YANKEE BRIDE, Jane Peart
#9  LIGHT OF MY HEART, Kathleen Karr
#10 LOVE BEYOND SURRENDER,
    Susan C. Feldhake
#11 ALL THE DAYS AFTER SUNDAY,
    Jeanette Gilge
#12 WINTERSPRING, Sandy Dengler
#13 HAND ME DOWN THE DAWN,
    Mary Harwell Sayler
#14 REBEL BRIDE, Jane Peart
#15 SPEAK SOFTLY, LOVE, Kathleen Yapp
#16 FROM THIS DAY FORWARD, Kathleen Karr

Watch for other books in the *Serenade Saga* series coming soon:
#17 THE RIVER BETWEEN, Jacquelyn Cook
#18 VALIANT BRIDE, Jane Peart